I'M
AFRAID,
YOU'RE
AFRAID

NO LONGER
PROPERTY OF
ROANOKE COUNTY LIBRARY

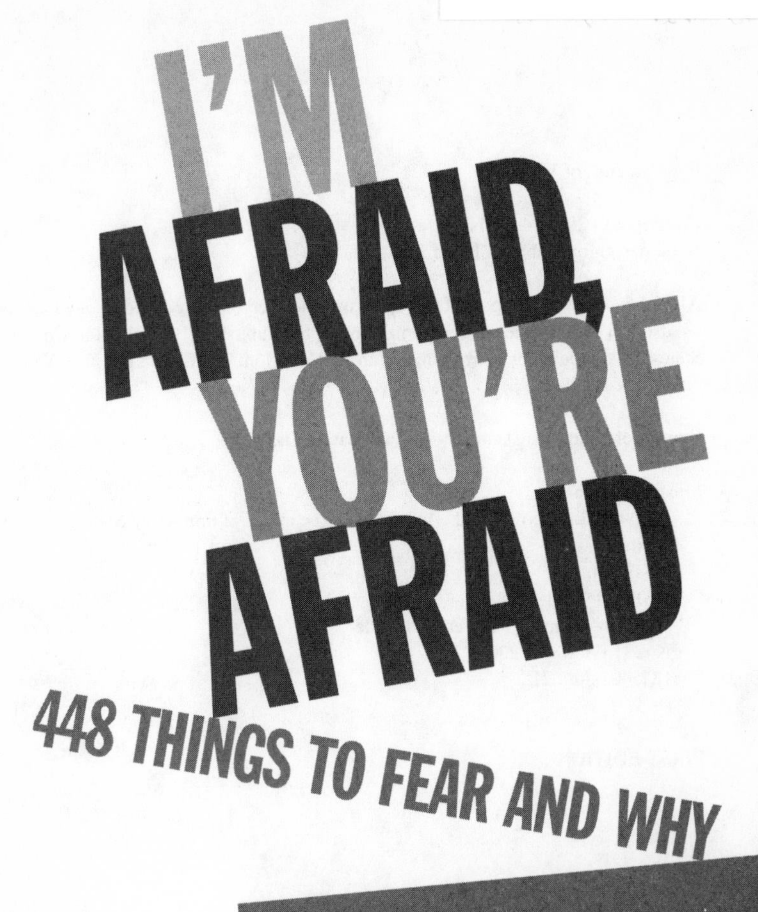
I'M
AFRAID,
YOU'RE
AFRAID
448 THINGS TO FEAR AND WHY

MELINDA MUSE

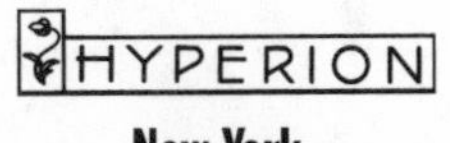
HYPERION

New York

For Dad and for Vance

Book design by Debbie Glasserman

 For information address: Hyperion, 77 W. 66th St., New York, New York 10023-6298.

Library of Congress Cataloging-in-Publication Data

Muse, Melinda.
I'm afraid, you're afraid : 448 things to be afraid of and why / Melinda Muse.—1st ed.
p. cm.
ISBN 0-7868-8395-2
1. Fear—Humor. 2. Fear. I. Title
PN6231.F4 M87 2000
818'.5402—dc 21 99-047622
CIP

FIRST EDITION

10 9 8 7 6 5 4 3 2 1

I'M
AFRAID,
YOU'RE
AFRAID

INTRODUCTION

Is it too much to ask, in the twenty-first century yet, that the world be a safer place than it was a hundred years ago? Even a bit so? Far from being the better, safer tomorrow of our dreams, the world, crazily enough, is a more dangerous place today than it was in grandma's day—in many ways, even in *her* grandma's day.

It's no longer survival of the fittest but of the wariest. One peek at public health, mortality, and accident statistics—amazing, nervous-making numbers—shows why we have every reason to be scared witless. From the natural catastrophes Mother Earth is heaving our way to mad cow disease, food-service filth, and dangerously lax import regulations, we have nowhere to run, nowhere to hide. Duck and cover—the Cowardly Lion's time has come!

I'm Afraid, You're Afraid is an encyclopedic compendium of the mad, bad, and dangerous—things that go bump, not only in the night but in broad daylight, too. From abstinence and alfalfa sprouts to yo-yos and parts-snagging zippers, it targets everything to be afraid of, and why.

You might consider this a textbook of life's hazards, one that specifies those vague rumblings you've had for years, fears you hoped were unfounded, fears that made you seem paranoid. Paranoid? At a time when goggled, rubber-gloved medical researchers are describing the horror-movie effects of flesh-eating bacteria and *Ebola* virus? When (again) it's Upton Sinclair's *Jungle* out there, with people dropping after eating name-brand fast food? When scientists have identified more than 2,000 asteroids and comets hurtling toward Earth? When global warming threatens to change world weather for the worst, and forever? Paranoid? You bet—stand tall and celebrate it!

Science and technology, unhelpfully enough, are only adding to our woes and worries, with so many of the conveniences we take for granted—from antibacterial soaps to jet propulsion—coming at a terrible price to our bodies, our serenity and to our planet. Just because we can make a supersonic car doesn't mean we should encourage even 70 mph on the nation's highways. Same goes for making blind dates on the Internet, gobbling down hormone supplements, experimenting with tropical plants in temperate zone gardens, and using cellular phones in restaurants: Such activities can sicken or kill you (in the last example, may even invite violence—and rightly so, some would say).

Many things today only appear to be safe, such as sports utility vehicles, which have a rollover rate that is two to three times that of passenger cars. The gas guzzlers only make you long for the comparatively reassuring days of the unsafe-at-any-speed Corvair and Pinto (banished to the junk heap a generation ago by Saint Ralph Nader).

You scoff, but a long-term Stanford University study proves that conscientious worry warts are likely to live longer than happy-go-lucky people. In a long-term (beginning in 1921) project, psychologists assessed the link between personality traits and mortality to find that, in any given year, the scaredy-cats were about 30 percent less likely to die than their carefree peers. So there.

I'm Afraid, You're Afraid won't let up until you hold your hands high in surrender. It's all here: Things you mustn't touch, places to flee, creatures and people to avoid. It's everything you should be afraid of under (and including) the sun. So don't be afraid to be afraid. And, more important, to laugh at your fears. Cock-eyed optimism is the tonic for a longer, healthier and—dare we hope—safer life.

Abstinence

Titter you may, but men who have frequent orgasms live longer than those who abstain from sex, says no less a source than the *British Medical Journal*.

Studying the link between frequency of sexual activity and incidence of death, Dr. George Davey-Smith asked 1,000 Welshmen, ages forty-five to fifty-nine, how often they had sex—daily, monthly, never? Ten years later, he analyzed death rates of the sample and found that men who engaged in sex at least two times a week lived twice as long as the less frequent lovers. Among possible explanations for the difference in life spans, Dr. Davey-Smith cited the hormonal effects that frequent ejaculations may have on the male heart.

If orgasms do reduce the risk of early death (a finding that could add meaning to the term "safe sex"), perhaps we can expect a new good-health homily: "A Lay a Day..."

Acne Medicine

As if having a zit eruption the night before that big job interview isn't worry enough, the Food and Drug Administration cites severe depression as a side effect of a powerful acne medication. The drug's manufacturer denies the FDA claim, saying that acne can cause depression all by itself.

The FDA wins. The pimple potion's new label (already slapped with a birth-defects warning) now reads, "may cause depression, psychosis and suicide."

Aerosol Containers

Any dunderhead knows that aerosol containers, under the right conditions—or wrong as it were—are mini Molotov cocktails. Still, emergency medics tend to people with frightful injuries, such as searing third-degree burns, corneal abrasions, and lung irritations—the painful results of container abuse. Each year, some 115 morgue-bound Americans do asinine things like poke holes in the containers, lob empties into open fires, or flick-a-Bic while spraying the high-pressure cans. Whoosh. Kapow!

All aerosol sprays contain fine particles that can hunker in the lungs and be absorbed into the bloodstream, and, depending on the chemicals, could be cancer-causing.

Don't wait to exhale; use a pump spray.

Afternoons

This could really screw up a happy hour. A twenty-three-year-long University of Washington study concludes that cardiac arrests occur just as often in the afternoon as in the morning, long considered the only peak time for heart attacks. The P.M. killer surge happens from about five o'clock to eight o'clock, just when you're kicking back with a martini, or kicking off, as the case may be.

(See *Daytime; Martinis; Mornings; Nighttime*)

Airplane Aisle Seats

Aisle be damned.

Next plane trip, forgo the tiny bit of extra leg room afforded by sitting on the aisle; instead, grab a window seat. Your noggin will appreciate the selfless gesture.

Overhead, a crammed luggage bin can pop open and suddenly spawn a rain of terror, spewing out suitcases, clunky camera bags, rock-heavy backpacks, wine cases, laptop computers, and golf clubs—just a few examples of the projectiles that assault some 4,500 air passengers every year. Head wounds, some leaving permanent brain damage, top the list of injuries, with briefcases the most common missile in the carry-on arsenal.

Airlines, which settle thousands of passenger injury claims each year, would welcome binless cabins. Flight attendants (suffering 15 percent of the in-flight injuries) justly squawk about the lax Federal Aviation Administration rules regarding tote-along baggage, which have gotten tougher after passengers tried (and failed) to bring on board a stuffed moose head, a mini refrigerator, a set of free weights, and incredibly, a big-screen television.

The former head of the National Transportation Safety Board and champion of fewer and lighter carry-ons, Jim Burnet, tells the *New York Times*: "The bins should be for hats and coats and light packages, like the souvenir sombrero you bring back from Acapulco." Olé.

(See *Frequent Flying*)

Alaska

It's a cold fact that, of all the states, Alaska holds the lead in death rates from unintentional injury, and is also the nation's most dangerous state for children. From 1986 to 1992, the injury death rate for youths aged nineteen or younger was 45.7 per 100,000, compared to the lower national rate of 30.2. Officials are stumped, failing to offer reasons for the high death rate of youngsters, but a good guess might include the zooming popularity of snowmobiling. Alaskans are dying in snowmobile accidents at least twice as fast as riders in any other state.

Alfalfa Sprouts

True or false? Alfalfa sprouts, the crunchy sandwich and salad fillers, are completely safe to eat. Ha! *Gut*cha!

The long-revered nutritional icons have been responsible for two major food poisoning outbreaks; the largest was in 1995, when an estimated 20,000 people fell ill and 1 person died after nibbling the springy add-ons. The gut of the problem is the way sprouts are cultivated. The warm, moist conditions that sprout alfalfa seeds can also breed pugnacious bacteria, like *E. coli* and salmonella. Even vigorous washings usually fail to rid the tangly sprouts of the repugnant germs.

The FDA and the U.S. Centers for Disease Control and Prevention ixnay sprout snacking by young kids, old folks, and people with weakened immune systems.

Alligator Shoes

Sounds like a crock, but consider changing into sneakers before heading off to the zoo. The *Europa Times* reports of the amorous moves made by a Mexico City wildlife park alligator on a tourist's alligator-skin boots. It was love at first sight but, alas for the gator, the star-crossed tryst was quickly thwarted by park wardens.

Aluminum Foil

Hi ow Silver!

The razor-sharp, serrated edges of aluminum foil boxes make a botch of fingers and hands. Every year, the U.S. Consumer Product Safety Commission's injury survey unfurls scores of bloody foil-dispenser episodes. Let this be a warning since many of the products' packages don't carry one.

Antennas

Must see clear TV? Fiddling around with rabbit ears could secure a lousy reception at the hospital. Every year, thousands of the antenna-attacked spend prime time on horizontal hold in emergency rooms, nursed for lacerated forearms and tongues, penetrated palates, punctured knees, and scratched corneas. Got the picture?

Apple Juice

Unpasteurized apple juice has caused bellyaching outbreaks of *E. coli* poisoning serious enough that the FDA now requires warning labels on the product. Drink juice—whatever the fruit—that's gone through the pasteurization process, a sure-fire bacteria killer.

(See *Grapefruit Juice; Juice Bars*)

Apricot Kernels

Quack quack. Apricot kernels don't cure cancer. Period. What they do, when chewed, is release the virulent poison cyanide. Turkey, a big apricot-growing country, has reported nine lethal poisonings directly attributable to kernel chewing; five cyanide poisoning cases in the United States during the 1970s stemmed from the wacky notion that apricot kernels were a viable cancer cure. The effects of nibbling the fruit kernels, depending on how much is ingested, range from dizziness to convulsions, coma, and death. Only a few years ago, a cyanide antidote had to be administered to save the life of a gasping-for-breath, kernel-snacking woman.

Lamenting the sale of apricot kernels as health food, an article in the *Annals of Emergency Medicine* describes the pits as "little cyanide pellets," and warns that an 8-ounce bag could kill up to six adults if consumed at one sitting.

Aromatherapy

Ah, the sweet smell of success.

Aromatherapy, the conceit of using essential oils to make you feel good from id to toe, reeks of enormous profits. The New-Agey mysticism cum hucksterism has flowered into a multi-million-dollar hype. Labels on soaps, shampoos, and creams, candles and lamps, massage lotions, shaving unguents, and jewelry vow to clear negative energies, increase your confidence, alleviate sorrow, relieve stress, and create a desire for peace. Oy.

Be nosy about what you whiff and rub on. Essential oils, extracted from flowers, plants, and herbs, are highly concentrated, volatile, and flammable. They react in different ways on people. Some oils produce uncomfortable side effects, others are plain dangerous. Essential oils from cinnamon, clove, nutmeg, and ginger can burn the skin; swallowing pennyroyal oil has caused miscarriages.

Too few studies have been done to prove or refute any scientific basis to aromatherapy's therapeutic claims. Since the FDA doesn't ride herd over the industry, use good scents. Do a skin patch test before anointing your body with the potent oils.

Artificial Nails

There's nothing bogus about the icky diseases that can be caused by wearing artificial nails. Bacteria creeping between natural nails and fake talons breed vile, hard-to-treat infections; fungi sprouts if moisture collects under the phony nails; smelly solvents, primers, and glues can set off skin-scorching allergic reactions. Break off a rigid artificial nail and your own fingernail is likely to be ripped from its nail bed. Ow, ow, ow.

Pediatricians hoist red flags about using nail primers around children. The products' toxic acid is blamed for giving kids more severe skin, eye, mouth, and lung burns than any other nail product. The FDA isn't wild about artificial nail products either, publishing health advisories that describe poisoning cases of young children.

Clip the faux paws.

Assertiveness

You probably don't care, but a dose of apathy is good medicine.

Experimenting with the notion that assertive behavior might be a tad detrimental to a person's health, Germany's University of Konstanz divided test subjects into two groups according to their personality traits. During performance tests, the gung-ho, ultra-responsible, aggressive assignment tacklers had much higher heart rates and blood pressures than did the passive, mellower slacker-type test takers.

What's to learn from these findings? Take-chargers, especially those with cardiac conditions, might be healthier by easing off the assertiveness act.

(See *Dominating Conversations*)

Astringents

Skin-toning astringents that remove facial oils and soap residue can cause complexion flare-ups. Dermatologists will tell you face-to-face to go easy on those cheeks; use mild formulations.

August

August wins hands down as the most dangerous month for accidents, with an average of 9,000 unintentional injuries, a leap from the usual monthly tally of 7,500. The dog days also lead the pack in the number of deaths every year in the United States from vehicle crashes and poisonings.

Autumn

Don't fall for the notion that spring is the only sneezeful season. Mold, dust, pet dander, holiday decorations, fireplace smoke, and, ugh, cockroach debris make autumn a miserable time of year for people with indoor allergies.

(See *Fallen Leaves; Spring; Summer; Winter*)

Baby-Faced Boys

Looks deceive. Baby-faced boys are more likely to be delinquent and commit more crimes than their less cherubic-looking pals, divulges a recent study that suggests that the sweet-appearing juvies intentionally try to derail their submissive image by acting naughty, not nice. The behavior of baby-faced girls, researchers note, isn't at all affected by their sugar-and-spice appearance.

Backpacks

School's in—time for reading and writhing as kids toddle off to class lugging backpacks that weigh as much as a third of their own weight. Crammed with texts, notebooks, school supplies, and athletic equipment, backpacks are causing big problems for little kids, as pediatricians grumble about children as beasts-of-burden.

Backpacks that tip the scales at more than 5 or 10 percent of a child's own body weight tilt him off balance. Forced to bend forward to support too much weight on his back, the loaded down kid must adopt an awkward posture that will eventually cause lower back pain.

More than 3,300 children, ages five to fourteen, were treated in emergency rooms in 1997 for injuries related to backpacks. It's not only the packs' poundage, but also how they're toted that causes one out of ten children to complain of back pain. Both straps should be worn so the pack is kept close to the body with its weight evenly distributed across the back and shoulders. Good advice as well for grown-up packers.

Bad Initials

BUMs and RATs don't live as long as VIPs and GODs, according to a University of California study that examined twenty-seven years worth of men's death certificates. Dr. Nicholas Christenfeld categorized the names of 5 million dead guys according to their initials. He then assigned the words that the initials spelled with the qualities of "good," "bad," or "neutral." The psychologist determined that people with good monograms like JOY, WOW and LOV lived more than 4.5 years longer than those in the neutral-monogram (WDW or JAY) category. Gents with bad tags, the DUDs and ASSes, died an average of almost 3 years earlier than the more neutrally initialed. SAD also is that people in the bad group—the APEs and PIGs—were more apt to commit suicide or die in an accident.

Dr. Christenfeld asserts that having "bad initials" is a lifelong negative psychological factor. It's a bummer to be called PIG but an ego boost to be recognized as ACE or WOW. The doctor says if a person holds the notion that "accidents aren't really accidents," then the lack of self-esteem may eventually lead to self-destructive behavior.

He could be DED right.

Bagels

From its once-humble Eastern European beginnings, the bagel has become an American staple. We nosh them out the wazoo—raisined, chocolate-chipped, loxed and cream-cheesed, sun-dried and tomatoed. It's a bagelapalooza!

Any way they're sliced, bagels are good eats—unless you're a klutz around the kitchen. Be careful. Cutting the slippery orbs can be very dangerous. An emergency medicine physician at George Washington University Medical Center refers to bagel cuts as the great underreported injury of our times.

To dissect a bagel safely: Lay it horizontally (*don't* stand it up) on a table or counter—never, ever hold it in your hand. Use a sharp, serrated knife to slice halfway through, then turn the bagel sideways and slice the rest of way. If the bagel's frozen, thaw it out before cutting it.

Baggy Pants

Hip-hop or trip-hop?

Loose-fitting, wide-legged trousers (more Emmett Kelley than haute couture) are toppling their wearers. The Consumer Product Safety Commission gripes about the urban-inspired fashion: A thirteen-year-old boy tripped on his billowing britches, tumbled down a flight of stairs and whacked his head open. A twenty-two-year-old construction worker was killed when his clown-sized pants got tangled in a moving tractor.

Don't be a fall guy. Lose the gangsta look.

(See *Tight Pants; Wearing Clothes*)

Baked Potatoes

Hold the tater trots.

Potatoes baked in aluminum foil caused the third-largest botulism outbreak ever reported, when in 1994, thirty people were stricken with the life-threatening toxin after eating potatoes prepared with a recipe for disaster. What happened was a lesson for us all.

Foil-shrouded potatoes were baked at 450° F for 2 hours, removed from the oven, and left sitting, still wrapped in the foil, at room temperature for 18 hours. Sounds safe enough, but there's a big biological hitch. Botulism-causing bacterial spores, festering in the soil and water, get on potatoes as they grow underground. High-temperature baking destroys the disagreeable bacteria—that is, unless the spuds are wrapped in foil, which traps in moisture and prevents the surface of the potatoes from getting spore-killing hot enough. Leaving the foiled tubers out at room temperature only encourages the nasty toxin to grow.

Baked potatoes have caused at least five other botulism outbreaks since 1978. Either put the foil-wrapped vegetables in the fridge or better yet, don't even use the silvery wrap. It's a silly way to bake them anyway.

(See *Aluminum Foil; Five Servings a Day; French Fries*)

Bakeries

Big commercial bakeries are such tarts! Pumping out tons of yeasty pollutants, clouding the sky with volatile compounds.

It's no loafing matter. As bread bakes, the atmosphere becomes one big chemistry set. Fermenting yeast produces carbon dioxide and ethanol (alcohol), which vaporizes, mixes with nitrogen, and when solar, humidity, temperature, and wind conditions are right, you get smog . . . not smelly and acrid but with the heavenly gauzy aroma of, well, baked bread.

Don't get your buns all hot crossed and bothered. The American Bakers Association isn't waffling about the problem; the trade group works with thirty-five states to devise more than pie-in-the-sky solutions to comply with federal clean air standards.

Baking Soda

Throw up or blow up? Your choice.

Baking soda's good for what ails a rocky tummy, but it's a remedy that could make you go belly up. Bicarbonate of sodium, a common household chemical that neutralizes indigestion-causing acid, has been responsible for the rupture of unusually full stomachs. The compound releases carbon dioxide gas into the stomach,

which much like a balloon, can reach a bursting point. There's a caution on baking soda boxes. Heed it.

Balloons

It was a real trial. The *British Medical Journal* tells of the man who, after blowing up twenty party balloons, went to the emergency room complaining of chest pains, of hearing crunching noises with every heartbeat, and of feeling air bubbles trapped under his skin. Sounds like a candidate for the psych ward, but E.R. docs made a quick diagnosis: the poor chap had burst some of the air sacs in his lungs, so that with each puff, he inflated himself a little bit more, a little bit more, a little bit more. The balloon man was treated and, within ten days, his symptoms had deflated.

Pop any notion to have latex balloons at kids' wingdings. The toys are second only to food as the most frequent cause of choking deaths, killing seven to ten children each year.

Banisters

The Consumer Product Safety Commission rails about banisters. In 1997, some 34,400 handrail-injured people were treated at hospital emergency rooms.

Slide rule: Watch where you're going.

(See *Elevators; Escalators*)

Bartending

Set 'em up, no, stick 'em up, Joe.

Bartenders are at high risk for becoming homicide statistics, with a murder rate of 3.5 per 100,000 workers, just under police officers' rate of 5.6.

Mixologists who toil in smoky bars also suffer respiratory problems, say University of California at San Francisco doctors, who examined fifty-three barkeeps before and after smoking was outlawed in California's watering holes. Before the ban, three-fourths of the men and women wheezed and coughed on the job, presumably from their exposure to long hours of secondhand smoke. In as little as a month after the state law went into effect, the bartenders' respiratory health improved, even if they still smoked themselves.

Bathing Suits

The tiny but wickedly venomous larvae of jellyfish, sea anemones, and coral can get trapped under bathing suits to sting the beach out of you. Seabather's eruption—skin lesions and pusy rash from the coastal critters—affects only areas of the body covered by swimwear.

Think thong.

(See *Beaches*)

Batteries

Common sense not included.

Fretful parents with tots who have crammed AAs up their nose or down their ear canals charge into emergency rooms every year for medical treatment. So do thousands of adults suffering with chemical burns from exploding batteries, wrenched backs from lifting too-heavy battery packs, and tummyaches after swallowing small, mistaken-for-vitamin-pills batteries.

Beaches

Beaches are vast sand traps, land-mined with tootsie-slicing debris, where even a minor cut becomes a major problem if bacteria-covered grit wiggles into the wound, a shore thing to become infected.

The coastline is reefer madness. Razor-sharp coral, ocean rocks, and seashells can be as painful as jellyfish stings, the most common marine injury to swimmers, snorkelers, and scuba divers, but watch out, too, for prickly sea urchins, scorpionfish, and spiny dogfish.

Beachophiles flop into beach chairs (flimsy furniture responsible for sending almost 6,000 people to E.R.s in 1997) to soak up melanoma-making UV radiation, all the while sun-scorching their eyeballs, already irritated by wind, sand, and salt water.

Wave so long to a cooling ocean dip. The surf could be fouled with untreated human waste, sewage overflow, septic tank discharge, chemical fertilizers, household toxics, and used motor oil. Record high numbers of swimming advisories and beach closings—75 percent higher in 1998 than in 1997—were the result of skyrocketing bacterial and pathogenic viral levels. According to a study published in *Epidemiology*, swimmers within 100 yards of storm drains who swallow the contaminated brine risk getting mighty sick with gastrointestinal illnesses and ear, nose, and throat infections.

All this pails in comparison to the hard luck of the North Carolina beachgoer who dug an 8-foot hole and crawled in for a little privacy. He got it. He suffocated when the sand pit caved in.

(See *Bathing Suits; Sunglasses; Sunlight; Sunscreen*)

Bean Bag Chairs

The days of macramé and eight-track tapes have long since passed, so why's that lump still sitting in your living room? No, not your brother-in-law. That godawful bean bag chair. Even putting aside the question of aesthetics (please don't), the plastic clots are a menace, especially to children. The Consumer Product Safety Commission is aware of five deaths and at least twenty-six nonfatal accidents (kids can crawl inside unzipped chairs and choke on the small foam-pellet filling). The guardian agency has

wisely recalled more than 12 million of the design-challenged chairs.

(See *Yard Sales*)

Beauty Parlors

Your hair day has gone from bad to omigod after spending three hours and a week's pay at the Cut 'n Curl. Lousy perm, botched bleach job, and the haircut from hell. You look terrible. What could be worse?

The "Beauty Parlor Syndrome" actually. The medical condition, as described by physicians, occurs when the action of dropping the head back over a shampoo sink tears the lining of the carotid artery, triggering a stroke. Unless you're dying for a totally new look, place a folded towel behind your neck to prevent a deadly dangle over the sink.

Between 3 P.M. and 4 P.M.

Where's the hickory stick when you need it? Half of all juvenile crime is committed after school on school days, with the most violent hour beginning at three o'clock. And the bad ones are in detention.

(See *Afternoons*)

Bible Quoting

Thou shalt not win. Hardly a top-ten commandment, but still one to heed in Dadeville, Alabama.

The Bible-quoting contest was heating up, with two competitors each reciting different renditions of the same verse. The dogmatic argument was settled when one of the contenders looked up the passage in the Good Book and discovered his version was wrong.

The sore loser—a backward Christian soldier—reached for his pistol and shot his opponent dead.

Bicycle Seats

It's a mounting problem, according to some doctors, while others think the cause for alarm is nuts.

Long bouts of cycling have been linked to male impotence by several urologists, who say that lengthy rides on narrow, pointed seats can compress arteries and nerves, which restricts critical blood flow to the penis. One doctor even went as far as to identify two kinds of cyclists: those who were already impotent and those who would become so.

Queasy riders, relax. Manufacturers are wheeling out new bikes with more crotch-friendly seats.

Bicycle Wheels

Blame about 6 percent of all bike mishaps on shoelaces, pants, purses, and bookbags that get tangled up in the wire wheels. Thus spoke the Consumer Product Safety Commission.

Birmingham, Alabama

Magnolias and accents drip in Birmingham. So do stomach acids. Tagged as the heartburn capital of the United States, 72 percent of the Southern city's residents suffer from the gastric Sturm und Drawl. It's nothing to burp at; an irritated esophagus can affect your sleep, your sex life, and general health.

(See *The South*)

Blow Dryers

Better locks next time.

Although the number of electrocutions from handheld hair dryers has fallen from an average of eighteen a year to fewer than four (attributed to tougher manufacturing standards and caution labels slapped on the products' electrical cords), the appliances still pose a danger. Long hair can be sucked into the hot-coiled dryers and set ablaze.

Blowing Off Steam

The pop psych notion of taking out your anger with a left jab to a pillow isn't as cathartic as it may seem; the fisticuffs will only make you more hostile.

The case against indulging rage is strong. Recent studies show that test subjects who were allowed to vent their anger by hitting a punching bag became more physically aggressive against rivals in subsequent competitive tests. Even more disturbing is that the subjects who first read articles that endorsed the effectiveness of venting-by-slugging were twice as combative toward other people.

Self-help books that advocate lashing out as a way to manage anger rather than by using calming relaxation methods are blowing steam up their assumptions.

(See *Bottling Up Anger*)

Blowing Your Nose

A vigorous nose blow elevates the blood pressure of the arteries and veins in the head, which could cause a stroke or rupture a blood vessel. Harness the honking, which will also help alleviate ear and sinus maladies.

(See *January*)

Blue Eyes

Seeing the world through baby blues may increase the chance of blindness. People with blue eyes which lack the sun-damage protecting pigment melanin, are more affected by macular degeneration.

After completing a four-year study of 3,600 people, Dr. Paul Mitchell of Australia's University of Sydney reports a twofold increased risk for blue-eyed people to suffer from the gradual and incurable disease that causes vision loss.

Body Odor

Lured by the irresistible scent of human perspiration, mosquitoes are especially bewitched by below-the-waist scents emitted by our apocrine sweat glands. Where you choose to spray insect repellant and deodorant remains a private matter.

(See *Deodorant*)

Bottled Water

It's everywhere.

Store-bought bottled water may not be as pure as the H_2O from your tap. An environmental advocacy group spilled the results of a four-year test of 103 brands of bottled water: Some of the pricey brands were contaminated with ornery bacteria and industrial chemicals, while other brands contained cancer-causing compounds, such as arsenic. A few bottled waters are loaded with major doses of sodium, and nowadays dentists suspect that kids are more cavity prone since they're swigging more bottled water, which lacks fluoride, a preventive measure for tooth decay.

Thirsty Americans, annually swilling an estimated 4.3 billion gallons of mineral water, spring water, distilled water, or just plain water water that's gone through extra filtration, have taken to worshiping the liter bottle as fetish, all the while turning up their noses at tap water. Truth is, municipal water supplies, scrutinized carefully by the Environmental Protection Agency and the Safe Drinking Water Act, are tested every day for disease-causing crud and chemicals, and utilities are required by law to provide consumers with annual water-quality reports. What's harder to swallow is that the pumped-up multibillion-dollar bottled-water industry, overseen by the FDA, is, more or less, self-regulated on an honor system, sets its own testing controls, and is under no regulatory requirement to disinfect or treat its water products for parasites.

No need to spring for the expensive stuff. The American Dietetic Association says that 85 percent of bottled water is actually municipal water anyway.

(See *Tap Water*)

Bottling Up Anger

Count to one, then let 'er rip.

Men of a certain age who have problems revealing their anger face a much higher risk of heart disease than do volcanic-tempered fellows, claims a British research team that, for nine years, studied almost 3,000 men between the ages of fifty and sixty-four. The risk of having a major coronary illness, like a heart attack, was 70 percent higher in men who couldn't express their rage. Study author Dr. John Gallacher says, "I think anger management is a serious issue." No kidding. The researcher cautions against expressing anger "willy-nilly," and suggests that men learn to deal with hostility-causing issues rather than toss tantrums at random.

(See *Blowing Off Steam*)

Bowing

Good manners, bad form.

The traditional Japanese greeting of bowing has been responsible for the deaths of at least twenty-four Tokyo residents. The how-do-you-doers succumbed from fatal head-cracking collisions on train platforms and escalators. Many other polite, but less seriously injured Japanese bowed and scraped themselves in revolving-door curtseys.

Really, a handshake will do.

Bowl Games

Are you ready for some football? Sure, as long as it's not a game of sudden death.

The sporty *New England Journal of Medicine* gives the play-by-play of the football fan who crawled out of the rack at noon on a New Year's Day, shuffled to his couch, and watched three consecutive bowl games on the tube. For more than 40 hours, the sofa spud stirred only for chow and potty breaks before hauling his lazy carcass back to bed. At work the next day, he experienced sharp chest pains and was rushed to the emergency room, where doctors diagnosed a blood clot in the slug's lungs brought on by the long hours of couch huddling.

Play it smart on game day—get up and run a few plays of your own every half hour or so.

(See *Football Games*)

Braids

Be careful how you do your do. Tight buns are better left to your derrière. Yanking hair into rubberband-trussed ponytails and twisting strands into tightly woven braids can damage delicate follicles, making your hair fall out. Heavy glass beads dangling from sleek, too-taut cornrows can also cause the tressful situation of hair loss.

Brassieres

It's a tempest in a D-cup.

Interviews with 4,400 women led two cultural anthropologists to proclaim that wearing a bra causes breast cancer. In their appraisal, the women who wore tight-fitting brassieres all the time, even to bed, had 125 times the breast cancer rate of the women who never crossed their hearts. Conversely, women who wore bras fewer than 12 hours a day decreased their cancer risk nineteen-fold. The researchers presumed that brassieres, by hindering the function of lymph glands in the breast, interfere with the elimination of cancer-causing toxins from the body.

The theory, never published in a reputable medical journal, nor reviewed by medical peer panels, hasn't earned much, if any, support from the medical community. Some physicians challenge the notion, considering it boobish, especially since the anthropological quest failed to incorporate correlative factors, such as the test subjects' smoking and dietary habits, genetic histories, or environmental surroundings.

It's not a Victorian secret that the first bra, with separate pockets for the breasts and hook-and-eye shoulder straps, was patented in 1893. Nowadays, with dozens of styles and sizes to choose from, it's important to select a well-fitting bra. Conforming to fashion can be deforming: Brassieres too tight, with narrow shoulder straps, especially on large-breasted women, can compress shoulder nerves, causing neurological damage to the neck, shoulders, and arms.

(See *Underwire Bras; Wearing Clothes*)

Bread

Bag that baguette. It could drive you mad.

Here's a little slice of life. Back in 1951, three people died immediately after eating bread from the local bakery in the French village of Pont Saint Esprit; fifty other bread eaters went insane, running through the streets yelling that they were being chased by animals. Some of the cuckoo villagers got toasted, committing suicide by jumping out of windows. Sounds like a really bad trip because that's what it was: the townsfolk were stoned.

Say what? The catch is in the rye. The rye flour used in the bread was contaminated with ergot, a fungus that contains the precursors of the hallucinogen LSD. The turn-on fungus was found in sorghum in the United States as recently as 1997, ergo, the name "party rye."

Brie

How do you solve a problem like listeria?

The wistful-sounding bacteria is anything but. Listeria sickens thousands of people every year, causing about 425 deaths, says the Centers for Disease Control and Prevention. The sneaky germ hovers in soil and water, and can eventually make its way into meats and dairy products, like brie, mozzarella, and feta. Symptoms of listeria poisoning—fever, muscle aches, nausea, stiff neck, and sometimes convulsions—can take up to 8 weeks to appear.

If you're healthy, there's little to stew about, but it's best for pregnant women, the elderly, and people with weak immune systems to spurn soft cheeses.

Brightly Colored Clothes

Seeking one human, M/F, S/M/D, juicy, no DDT; reply to Nest 17.

Not to get personal, but you're likely to be bitten by smitten bees, wasps, and hornets if you insist on wearing brightly colored clothes that advertise what a tasty hotty you are.

(See *Dark-Colored Clothes*)

Brush Cutters

Brush cutters mean business. With steel blades that can easily and efficiently whack off an arm, leg, or hand, the mondo yard tools pose the greatest danger not to operators but to bystanders. The hazard exists in working the blade too close to a fence or building, which can ricochet a cutter out of control, like it did for one man, whose nearby wife was torn asunder; the vibrating tool sliced into her thigh, then nearly amputated her left hand. Yeeowwww. Before revving up anything with steel blades, read the instructions and shoo away anyone close by.

(See *Yard Work*)

Bubble Baths

A frothy bubble bath can irritate a female's external genitalia. The chemical ingredients can burn, itch, and crack the vulval skin, and even enter the vagina to cause painful bladder infections.

Scud the suds.

Bug Zappers

You swat and fumigate, and nothing works. Every insect within a 10-mile radius dive-bombs your backyard cookout. Time to plug in the heavy artillery. Zap! Pop! Crackle! Dead bug sizzling.

Bug zappers are mean killing machines, and admit it, you get a charge hearing that *zzzt, zzzt, zzzt.* But 99 percent of the crispy critters that reach electronic nirvana—nearly 71 billion are fried each month—turn out to be innocent nonbiters, like harmless beetles and beneficial but doomed moths that flutter to the sirens of ultraviolet rays, mistaking the soft glow for navigational moonlight. Blood-sucking mosquitoes, oblivious of the zapper's pyrotechnic lure, cruise on past the death trap to hone in on your juicy, carbon dioxide–emitting neck.

Zappers do barbecue nasty common house flies. Good riddance, you cheer. Not really; when the flies, yucky with human and animal wastes, explode, millions of bacteria are hurled into the air, some tossed as far as 6 feet away. Pass the potato salad.

Dr. James Urban, professor of biology at Kansas State University, thinks that bug zappers are a bad, disease-spreading idea and suggests using fly paper inside and a birdhouse outside to attract insect-eating birds.

C

Camping

Some people enjoy sleeping out under the stars—campers, they call themselves. Knuckleheads is more like it.

The development of shelter was a great leap forward in human development, so why is it that otherwise enlightened human beings will pitch tents in beds of poison ivy? Tempt bears and other hungry beasts with campfire aromas? Forgo hygiene? Or (with intrusive, heat-seeking scorpions and snakes) snuggle in sleeping bags—which may as well be called body bags. Pure atavism, that's what it is, an ill-advised regression to our unevolved selves, to before we walked on two legs and built nice roofs over our heads.

Wilderness gear only adds to the danger (and expense) of camping, offering a bogus sense of readiness. Propane lanterns and stoves, charcoal grills, tent stakes and rigging—all are implements of disaster. According to a recent study, your chances are much greater—by more than three to one—for getting injured around a campsite than by rappelling down a rock face. One poor city slicker on a back-to-nature holiday with his wife and three children started the weekend in the Great Smoky

Mountains by gashing his ankle on the Swiss Army knife that had slipped from his belt into his hiking boot. A few hours later, the tinhorn punctured a buttock (his own) by sitting on a tent stake. That night, a flame leaped from the campfire to the "fireproof" tent, promptly setting it and all their supplies ablaze. Happily, the unhappy campers survived to tell the tale and (much later) laugh about it.

If traveling together is a test of relationships, camping is the final exam: it's very easy to despise the snorer whose tossing and turning brings down the tent, who drinks more than a fair share of the potable water, who leaves graham crackers out for the bears, and who forgets to pack the toilet paper. Cumbayah.

If bivouacking took one far away from urban dangers, it might score a point in its favor. But that's not the case, as state and national parks, beaches and other public campgrounds experience severe crowding and rising crime rates. Hordes of people trek to America's 378 national parks. Yearly visits by more than 300 million tourists have overwhelmed the park system's infrastructure: The parks are falling apart and desperately need billions of dollars to repair years of overuse, neglect, and vandalism. It would take $46 million just to fix up Yellowstone National Park, tagged by a parks advocacy group as the "poster child for neglect." The problems are widespread—traffic congestion, air pollution, poor maintenance, and inadequate safeguards against personal danger and property destruction.

Budget cuts have reduced the number of park rangers, leading to slower response times to emergencies, increases in the killing of wildlife, thefts, weapons charges, and motorist violations. Rangers do their best to protect visitors, but still, in 1998, the National Park Service reported 146 deaths and 6,638 search-and-rescue efforts. Arrgh, Wilderness.

Sleeping bags? Collapsible toilets? Freeze-dried dinner? Thanks all the same, but you might be better off risking a night at a fleabag motel.

(See *Hotel Rooms; Marshmallows; Sleeping Bags*)

Candles

Wickedly popular, candles are a bazillion-dollar industry. Light them to spark romance, hold vigils, or cast spells; just don't get waxed.

In 1996, candles caused nearly 10,000 fires (an 82 percent increase from 1990), and were responsible for 126 deaths. Hundreds of millions of dollars in property damage and human injury can be avoided by never, ever leaving candles unattended.

Give a good blow before you go.

Canned Tuna

Flipper is out of harm's way, but you may not be. Labels on cans of tuna smugly assure a dolphin-free meal, but some don't list a preservative found in much of the tinned fish sold in American stores. Sulfites can cause swollen tongues, closed throats, and even life-threatening shock in people allergic to the chemical substances.

(See *Dolphins*)

Can Openers

Bacteria form a conga line on the way to feast on food-encrusted can openers. Be a killjoy; bombard the thugs with a dose of bleach. And be careful operating the handy device; it's supposed to open cans, not flesh wounds.

Cardboard Boxes

Toxic molds could be colonizing right now in your attic or basement, marshaling forces to plague you with migraines, chronic fatigue, itchy eyes, and flu symptoms.

Poisonous fungi (which look exactly like the innocuous crud on your shower curtain) thrive in wet areas and consider cellulose, the stuff of cardboard boxes, a movable feast. *Stachybotrys, Aspergillus,* and *Penicillium* are the molds most likely to cause health problems, and should be purged, pronto, with a dose of chlorine bleach. For big fungal patches—more than 1 to 2 feet square—call in a hired gun who's better equipped for the clean-up.

Careers in Advertising

They seem such glam jobs. Photo shoots in exotic locales, supermodels, gray flannel suits. But the truth in advertising is that its employees should receive hazard pay since more of them—sixteen, according to the Bureau of Labor Statistics—died on the job in 1995 than did electrical repair workers (fifteen), petroleum refiners (thirteen), and car factory employees (six).

Half of the hucksters died in transportation accidents; none, however, was slaughtered on avenues, Madison or otherwise.

Car Phones

Put a towing company on speed dial.

Gabbing on a car phone is as dangerous as drinking and driving, claims a University of Toronto study that links the chatty multitasking to a fourfold increase in collisions. Most bang-ups occur while drivers are in the middle of conversations; the distraction is the chitchat itself, not the dialing or answering or holding the instrument.

Phoney driving has been banned in Japan, Spain, Brazil, and parts of Australia. Even New York City cabbies have been ordered off the hook. But a recent trend in the United States should ring some bells. Thanks to lower service costs and aggressive marketing campaigns, a growing number of teenagers are yakking on car phones. Teenage drivers have extremely high rates of both fatal and nonfatal crashes compared with drivers of other ages. Do the math.

(See *Sixteen-Year-Old Drivers*)

Car-Pool Lanes

Car-pool lanes were designed to allow vehicles with two or more occupants to zoom ahead of single-driver cars. The best laid plans...

What was touted to be the salvation of traffic-snarled drivers has often proved to be an expensive bust. In some cities, high-occupancy vehicle lanes are nothing but empty, poorly planned ribbons of asphalt. Some transportation experts estimate that 60 percent of the nation's HOV lanes are underused. Just as well; maneuvering into position to enter the speedy lanes requires the skills of a stock-car driver—zigzagging across multiple lanes of heavy traffic, cutting in front of other drivers to jockey into position. Once you're there, cruising in the zippy byway can get really hairy if the fast lane's not separated from the slower ones by some type of barrier; you're HOVing along at 65 mph when alongside in the pokey lane, a fed-up trucker decides hellwithit, and whips his 18-wheeler out in front of you. Not much wiggle room.

Some cities have opted to lower the car-pool lanes' designated number of people to as few as two, while other municipalities, recalling the hare and tortoise morality tale, have scrapped car-pool lanes altogether.

Car Windows

Car windows don't block out the sun's long-range ultraviolet rays that, over time, wizen your skin.

Avoid road age. Apply UVA-protective film to car windows.

Cartoons

Researchers, with a little too much time on their hands, screened fifty animated films released between 1937 and 1997 and determined that in two-thirds of them, villains and (gasp!) heroes alike used alcohol or tobacco. The messages were subtle and brief (taking up, on average, about 1.5 minutes in a full-length feature) but even so, none of the movies explicitly stated that smoking and drinking were bad-for-you behaviors.

The loony toon assessment failed to explore whether the portrayals actually lead to kiddy substance abuse. "It's a stretch," says Houston child psychologist, Dr. Dolores McKellar. "The study, which suggests that fleeting shots of smoking and drinking by cartoon characters set the stage for current problems of drug abuse, ignores many other possible variables and intervening events."

A popular cartoon show in Japan did have a dire effect on its viewers a few years back. A five-second scene using flashing red lights for a character's eyes induced epileptic-like convulsions in more than 700 tooners. The show's producers agreed to never again broadcast the seizure-causing strobe effects.

Casinos

Lousy odds. Only 150 of the 736 high rollers who had heart attacks in Las Vegas casinos during a recent 42-month period lived to place another wager. Paramedics, having to maneuver around the throngs in the mammoth gaming halls, averaged 11 minutes to reach the crapped-out victims, oftentimes too late to jump-start their bum tickers. Hedging their bets, many casinos have installed defibrillators to help restore heart-stopping cardiac rhythms until medical help arrives.

Casseroles

Deep dish = deep doo doo.

Keeping a casserole in the refrigerator can be iffy. Food in the center of a deep-dish container may not cool fast enough to stop bacteria from doing what bacteria do best—multiplying. Before shoving a casserole in the fridge, divide the leftovers and put them into shallow containers so they'll cool down quickly and limit the growth of pesky germs.

Cats

Cat-scratch fever. Good song, bad disease. A skin-breaking kitty-claw swipe can jump-start a flulike infection, giving the scratchee swollen lymph nodes and a fever that antibiotics must quell. Cat bites, as a whole, are more dangerous than dog bites because they're usually deep puncture wounds and become infected about 40 percent more often than Fido's nips.

(See *Dogs; Hedgehogs; Lizards; Parakeets*)

Cereal

Only dull people are brilliant at breakfast.—Oscar Wilde.

Surveys tell us that most Americans reach for cereal for the morning meal. It's a healthy way to start the day as long as the cereal box was tightly closed to keep out freeloading rodents and roaches. Cestodiasis is an infection, affecting mainly children, caused by a tapeworm that's transmitted to people who've eaten food infested with rat fleas or cockroach droppings. Hardly the breakfast of champions.

Can't really call it a cereal killer but one brand of toasted oats did make people extremely sick in a 1998 outbreak of salmonella. With forty people hospitalized and a couple hundred others laid low with fever and stomach cramps, the Centers for Disease Control and Prevention blew the whistle on the tainted oats.

Chain Saws

"It's like grabbing a hand grenade without a pin in it." That about says it all. And who better to kvetch about what he calls the most dangerous hand tool than fifth-generation logger U.S. Forest Service technician Carl Smith, who says it's plain foolishness that a license and special training aren't required to operate a chain saw.

Carl's right. Chain saws, used primarily to trim branches and cut logs, are a menace and cause an average of 40,000 injuries every year. Improvements over the years have made the tool lighter (easier to lug up tall trees), sharper, and more powerful, putting users at greater risk for grisly wounds. If the tip of the saw's cutting bar catches a piece of wood the wrong way, it's likely to throw the whirring bar back toward the soon-to-be-mangled sawer.

To make sure the limbs you whack off aren't your own, read the instruction manual. Wear a hard hat and safety glasses, and since most chain saw injuries happen below the waist, protective leg chaps and high-top, steel-toed boots are *de riguer*. Many saws whine at 118 decibels, equivalent to the noise of an *Apollo* rocket liftoff, so earplugs are a must. Pull on a pair of thick gloves; a chain saw's constant vibration can damage blood vessels and impair circulation. One more thing: keep a first-aid kit handy.

(See *Earplugs; Yard Work*)

Chamomile Tea

There was an Old Man of Vienna,
Who lived upon Tincture of Senna;
When that did not agree,
He took Chamomile Tea,
That nasty Old Man of Vienna.

The dyspeptic coot in Edward Lear's nineteenth-century limerick snacked on flower-powered concoctions to cure his ills. Today, scads of herb-happy Americans are following suit, making the botanical market a blooming $12 billion industry. But manufacturers of herbal potions, pills, and teas are unregulated, not obliged in the least to meet any government or industry standard for safety or effectiveness.

Don't be a chump. Just because herbs are "natural" doesn't mean they're safe to ingest (to wit: Socrates' hemlock cocktail). Some have dangerous side effects, while others are simply ineffective and a waste of money. Do some homework before you pharmaceutically soothe your soul, calm your nerves, or boost your sex life.

Chamomile tea? For the ragweed allergic, a few sips of the brew can cause hives or mild respiratory problems, or even kill as it did a few years back when a thirty-five-year-old woman went into anaphylactic shock after tipping back her teacup.

Champagne

Don't get corkscrewed. When opening champagne, aim the bottle of bubbly away from your face (and anyone else's). Ophthalmologists caution about projectile corks, small enough to bypass eye-protecting facial bones and slam into eye sockets.

Cheerleading

Gimme an O! Gimme a U! Gimme an O-U-C-H!!

High school sporting events are bone-breaking, muscle-pulling, cartilage-ripping fun for the whole family—and that's just the rough-and-tumble action on the sidelines. Cheerleaders are almost as likely to wind up on the injury list as the athletes they root for. Airborne cartwheels, skyscraping human pyramids (banned by many schools as too dangerous), tumbling routines at breakneck speed—crowd-pleasing acrobatics, to be sure, but the showmanship is taking its toll.

The pepsters are somersaulting to physicians in record numbers. Orthopedic surgeon Dr. Carey Windler of the Austin Sports Medicine Clinic says, "Cheerleading now involves dramatic and dangerous gymnastic moves that have the potential for significant injuries to the head, back, and neck, as well as for the more common ankle and knee complaints."

In 1996, the National Cheerleaders Association reported more than 6,000 injuries sustained by members of high school yell squads. On average, high school cheerleaders lost 28.8 days after an injury, compared with high school football players who returned to the playing field after only 5.6 days of recuperation.

(See *Football Games*)

Chewing Gum

The medical journal *Pediatrics* smacks an alarm about a wad of chewing gum health hazards, ranging from causing cavities to, if swallowed, intestinal blockage. Sweeteners in sugarless gum can launch diarrhea and flatulence; cinnamon gum has been linked to mouth ulcers; bubble gum can inflame mouth linings; licorice gum might raise blood pressures; and, no matter what the flavor, sticky chewing gum can pluck out fillings, crowns, and bridges.

Cleaning up gum residue from private and public facilities exacts enormous financial costs. Gum pollution, or gumfitti, as it's called, requires the use of potent removal solvents, which could have bad environmental consequences.

Chewing's a tacky habit: Many airports don't sell gum because of the high cleanup costs; Singapore's a real stickler—try to bring gum into the no-nonsense country and you're busted.

(See *Cinnamon Gum*)

Chilies

You'll be a pepper too. Red or green, tongue-torching chili peppers can burn the skin of people sensitive to the active ingredient, capsaicin, fiery enough to be used in mugger-thwarting Mace spray.

Chopsticks

How do you say Maalox in Mandarin?

Eating family style in China means everyone at the table reaches with chopsticks into the same bowls. If one person is infected with *Helicobacter pylori*, the ulcer-causing bacteria, the familial chopsticking will spread the organism to other diners.

Christmas

The prospect of Christmas appalls me.—Evelyn Waugh

You better watch out. Christmas is that special time of year, the season for the opening of gifts and wounds; for hall decking with boughs of allergy-causing, poisonous greenery; of back-straining package lifting; for overindulging in booze and migraine-triggering foods; of wheezing asthma attacks from fresh-cut Christmas trees, which, by the way, cause an average of 600 fires and 33 deaths every year; for hand-slicing glass ornaments; of expensive doctor visits for toy-related injuries (more than 141,000 in 1997); for family gatherings around a salmonella-poisoned dinner table. Is it any wonder that in 1996, *Prevention* magazine found that most people rank the holidays as more stressful than their last job interview? Joy to the world.

Next to having to endure hours of sappy holiday TV specials, Christmas's most nerve-wracking ritual is gift buying. Hazardous, too. A British investigation shows that male stress levels skyrocket—equal to that of police officers going into dangerous situations—when they are confronted with crowded stores (especially those that play loud music), then are forced to choose gifts and stand in check-out lines. More than 70 percent of the shopping wusses recorded abnormal vital signs even before leaving their houses.

'Tis the season of the heart—burn and attack. More than a quarter of the American population suffers the digestive agony of holiday heartburn, and more heart attacks occur during December and January, peaking in the festive season between Christmas and New Year's. The fa-la-la holiday can also be a heartbreaker; for many people, loneliness and despair overshadow the seasonal joys. But Christmas has gotten a bad rap when it comes to suicide: December actually records fewer suicides than any other month.

Chubby Cheeks

Baby's got back. Sexy. But those paunchy jowls are something else.

Plump cheeks could signal more body fat and a higher risk for complications of obesity, puffs *The New England Journal of Medicine*.

(See *Fat Necks; Long Faces*)

Cigars

Meet spokesmodel Gabby Hayes.

Puffing on a stogie looks silly enough; try it with no teeth. Men who smoke cigars run a much greater risk of tooth loss, periodontal disease, and jaw bone deficiencies than nonsmokers, says the Boston University School of Dental Medicine.

Cigar smoking, "the most obnoxious fad of the 90s" according to *Spy* magazine, is a pretentious symbol of the good life (and if it's all the same, let's not get into the Freudian aspects); it's also a cancer-mongering habit. One cigar, with as much tobacco as a pack of cigarettes, generates at least seven times as much tar as one cigarette, eleven times the carbon monoxide, and four times as much nicotine.

Cigar smokers, or aficionados as they prefer to be called,

are twice as likely to get mouth, throat, and lung cancers as nonsmokers, and are more disposed to develop heart disease or chronic obstructive pulmonary disease. Those snazzy, too-cool cigar bars should offer free respirator hookups to their patrons.

Cinnamon Gum

The active ingredient in cinnamon-flavored gum, candy, and breath mints is the allergen cinnamic-aldehyde, which can cause white spots and sores to erupt in the mouth.

(See *Chewing Gum*)

City Biking

Two-wheeled maneuvering on city boulevards has become a spoiled sport; bike-riding fatalities have spiked almost 30 percent in the last five years. Accidents involving bicycles, from the very minor to near-fatal, have increased by more than 10 percent. True, a lot more bikers are on the streets, but there's an SOB factor in play: all too often vehicle-driving creeps tailgate and sideswipe cyclists, or get their kicks from chunking beer cans at the two-wheelers.

You already have the advantage over the behind-the-wheel nitwits. You've got a brain. Protect it: Wear a helmet.

Classical Performances

Mozart has the most heart. Researchers, after studying the patient load at first-aid stations at 405 different musical venues—categorized as either classical, country, jazz and blues, light/easy listening, rock or other (gospel/Christian, Latin, rap and world)—over a five-year period, determined that classical performances had the highest likelihood of audience members having heart problems, like cardiac arrest, during the concert.

(See *Gospel Concerts; Rock Concerts*)

Cleanliness

Enough already! Stop with the antibacterial products and microbe shields, heavy-duty disinfectants, and antiseptic cleansers. It's germ warfare and we're losing the battle.

Superduper cleansers are crowding store shelves. Germ-killing soaps, sponges, sprays, cutting boards, bed linens, toothpastes, even fabrics and toys are increasingly part of a household's antiseptic arsenal. It's a wicked world all right, plump with billions of microorganisms—some good, some bad—but many scientists fear America's hypervigilant cleanliness obsession is only encouraging menacing pathogens to mutate, speeding up the rate at which bacteria learn to combat antibiotics, which will ultimately promote resistant strains of Übergerms.

Best way to stay in the pink? Simple. Wash your hands. Before and after eating, handling food, and having sex. Scrub with soap, any kind, and water before treating a wound and after using the toilet, sneezing, blowing your nose, changing a diaper, gardening, or playing with a pet. Simple.

Close Shaves

Face-scraping shaves can give what's called barber's itch, a pimply, madly itchy rash that's caused by bacteria or a fungus. Shaving cream may not be much help if you're allergic to color additives or perfumes. For a cut above the rest, sport a beard.

(See *Gray Beards; Mustaches*)

Clothespins

Laundry day can leave you hung out to dry. About 3,000 people sought emergency medical attention in 1997 for scalp lacerations, corneal abrasions, ankle sprains, bruises, and cuts from clothespins and clotheslines.

(See *Laundry*)

Coffee Cups

It's alive! Curious researchers at the University of Arizona brewed up a study to discover if office coffee cups were clean and found that 40 percent of the mugs were brimming with bowel-churning *E. coli* and coliform bacterias. Sloppy dishwashing techniques took the heat for the grossness. If it's not the jolt you crave from a java fix, scrub your cup in hot, soapy water.

Cold Weather

Gloomy forecast: an increased risk of heart attacks related to extreme changes in atmospheric pressure.

French researchers discovered that when the temperature dropped 18 degrees for a particular day, the chances of a man suffering his first heart attack on that day jumped 13 percent. The study also showed that relatively sharp temperature changes increased the likelihood of a second heart attack by 38 percent. Other studies have linked cold weather with increases in blood pressure, a rise in blood clots, and a hike in blood fats.

(See *Winter*)

Contact Lenses

Jeepers creepers, where'd you get those eight balls?

Contact lenses that transform eyes into bizarre orbs—smiley

faces, stars and stripes, dollar signs—are hot items on the black market. Teens can buy the goofy-looking lenses through classified ads, a practice that drives eye specialists bonkers. The doctors fret about bacterial infections, allergic reactions, abrasions, and corneal ulcers that can be triggered by the the unprescribed and unfitted lenses. The American Academy of Ophthalmology comes down hard on the practice and cautions that wearing the decorative lenses—no matter the source—may interfere with sight-crucial activities, like driving a car.

Swapping costume lenses among friends is very trendy too, but kids, as usual, aren't terribly farsighted about the fad; lens sharing spreads bacteria, viruses, fungi, and amoebas that cause eye diseases, even blindness.

See straight to follow precautions, no matter what kind of contacts you wear. Lenses left in too long, carelessly cleaned, or wet with saliva or tap water can scar the cornea and permanently impair vision. And, don't ever forget to take them out, the *British Medical Journal* reminds, reporting the case of an absent-minded woman who complained of eye pain until doctors removed a rigid gas permeable lens that had been lodged in her left eyelid for six years.

(See *Eyeglasses*)

Cook-in-the-Bag Foods

Barf-in-the-john foods is more like it, if you follow cooking instructions on some cook-in-the-bag foods. Slowly heating refrigerated cook-in-the-bag meals, such as beef stew or stuffed pasta, may encourage the *E. coli* bacteria to adapt to intense heat. Investigators at the Agricultural Research Service tested samples of the convenient cook-in-the-bag foods and determined that when slowly heated to about 115° F for 15 to 30 minutes, the food harbored *E. coli* that was 50 percent more resistant to high temperatures that otherwise would kill it.

Cookbooks

Recipes should toss in a dash of common sense. A 1977 cookbook was whisked out of the market by its publisher in a stew about one of its custard recipes that instructed readers to cook an unopened can of condensed milk in a crockpot for four hours. Yep, milk cans detonated, showering kitchens with shards of crockpot glass. Yet another cookbook recalled from store shelves provided the heart-stopping hint of decorating cakes with lily of the valley, a poisonous flower that can cause circulatory problems.

Cookie Dough

Lots of grown-ups never get over the childhood pleasure of eating raw cookie dough. But the Proustian indulgence can cause gastrointestinal upset. The culprit is the notorious salmonella bacteria nesting in some raw eggs, an essential ingredient in most cookie dough recipes.

Still have to lick the bowl? Whip up a batch using an egg substitute product. Or buy the frozen slice-and-bake variety, made with pasteurized eggs. It may taste like sweet Play-Doh, but you won't toss your cookies.

Cookie Sheets

Folks with certain food allergies could find themselves in a sheetload of trouble if remains of one food, like peanuts or chocolate, contaminate another. Get out the scouring pad and clean utensils and cookware well after each use.

Cookware

Panhandlers take note: heated on high temperatures, aluminum cookware can melt. An alert from the Consumer Product Safety

Commission cautions about burns from dripping molten aluminum.

Coping

Coping is highly overrated. "It brings bad stuff," pouts Cornell University's Dr. Gary Evans in *Psychology Today*. The psychologist says that when we manage to overcome our problems, it may only generate more trouble. For instance, when children live in a noisy flight path, they adjust to the overhead racket by learning to tune it out, which seems like a sensible way to deal with the situation, but, at the same time, the kids turn a deaf ear to speech and language acquisition. People who reside in extremely crowded conditions create their own personal space and learn to cope by withdrawing from others, which isn't, according to the doctor, a healthy nudge toward developing supportive, healthy personal relationships.

Cosmetic Counters

The new shades are in! Pathogenic Pink. Sullied Sienna. Bacterial Berry.

An FDA probe discovered that more than 5 percent of cosmetic-counter makeup samples were corrupted by fungi, molds, and other organisms. Every time an eye shadow case or jar of foundation is opened, noxious bacteria scurry in. By testing a cosmetic on your mouth or eyes rather than your hand, there's a slim chance of catching a cold, the herpes virus, a staph infection, or an intestinal bug from the sicko who dabbed it on before you.

Coworkers

It's far more likely your colleagues will go preschool rather than postal.

Let's tattle on the out-of-control jerks who bite, punch and twist the arms of their coworkers. The Bureau of Labor Statistics annually records nearly 1,000 bites; more than 2,000 squeezes, pinches, and scratches; and almost 10,000 incidents of kicks and bops to the head and torso—all from workplace squabbles.

Picking fights is not a highly effective habit; violence-at-work victims cost employers at least $3.6 billion a year in lost time and health claims.

Cracking Knuckles

Say, "Excuse me." When you crack your knuckles, you're actually passing gas. Pushing a finger joint in or out of its normal position displaces gases, mostly carbon dioxide, from the joint space, causing the popping sound. All this bending and twisting puts a lot of stress on the ligaments and tendons that hold the knuckle together. Years of "finger flatulence" could roughen and inflame the joint surfaces; some studies have associated frequent knuckle cracking with early arthritis. Break the crack habit.

Crayons

Up your nose with Dusty Rose. Color minor most of the crayon-related trips to the emergency room, where doctors extract the sticks of tint from kids' ear canals and nasal passages—some 2,100 in all during 1997. But sketch some hospital visits more worrisome—treatment for the likes of scratched corneas and, following a waxy nibble, serious allergic reactions.

Croquet

You think it's a wimpy game for linen-wearing, sherry-sipping wienies who swack colorful balls through wire hoops.

Oh yeah? Croquet's more wicket than you think. A survey of English croquet players from Newcastle upon Tyne, England (where else?) reveals that 35 percent of the mallet wielders sustained at least one injury to the hand, wrist, or forearm. Hurt worse were the players slinging newfangled fiberglass mallets rather than the traditional wooden ones.

Crossing Your Legs

Charm school be damned. Sitting with crossed legs could lead to varicose and spider veins. Spread 'em.

Crying

A sob story could set off a migraine. Crying jags brought on by sadness or emotional turmoil trigger the searing headaches in some people. The journal *Headache* says that peeling onions or shedding happy tears doesn't have the same sickening boo-hoo effect.

(See *Stemming Tears*)

Crystal Ware

About 30 percent of elegant, expensive crystalware is lead, which gives it brilliance and heftiness but may leach into any liquid held in a glass or decanter. Nerve damage, mental disorders, heart and kidney problems can stem from lead if ingested in significant amounts. Some manufacturers stopped producing crystal baby bottles and have encouraged consumers to buy crystal ware only for decorative use.

Curling Irons

By twists and turns of product improvements, curling irons now get very, very hot, and they're burning too many kids. From 1985 through 1988, approximately 6,400 children under five years of age suffered burns severe enough to be treated in emergency rooms. Hot-wand eye injuries of young women between fifteen and twenty-four years old accounted for a few thousand more hospital visits. Straighten up. Lock yours away.

Cut Grass

New-mown lawns give off chemicals like methanol, acetaldehyde, and acetone—volatile chemical compounds that don't do much to improve the Earth's increasingly crummy air quality. On a greener side, scientists in the journal *Geophysical Research Letters* claim that the weekend chore probably isn't toxic to individuals, so there's no reason not to get off your grass and start shearing it.

(See *Yard Work*)

Cutting Boards

Let's cut cheese, er, to the chase.

The germ-meister himself, microbiologist Dr. Charles Gerba of the University of Arizona, claims a food-scabby cutting board has a hundred times more colon-rocking bacteria than does a toilet seat. Unless you plan on serving canapés à la commode, clean your cutting board each time you use it and, every so often, wipe it down with a spot of bleach.

Dallas–Fort Worth

Hey! If it's so big, why's everybody in Texas running into one another? Three of the nation's ten most dangerous intersections are in the Dallas–Fort Worth area, with a traffic-clogged corner in suburban Dallas ranked number one, tallying 263 crashes in 1998. Rounding out the list are three intersections in car-choked California, and others in the Chicago and Detroit areas; Clearwater, Florida; and Las Vegas.

The DFW area is also ranked eighth in the nation in fatalities attributed to aggressive driving. Whoa, cowboys!

Dark-Colored Clothes

Seeking one human, M/F, S/M/D, juicy, no DDT; reply to Stagnant Pool 25.

Not to get personal, but you're likely to be bitten by smitten mosquitoes if you insist on wearing dark-colored clothes that advertise what a tasty Goth you are.

(See *Brightly Colored Clothes*)

Daylight Savings Time

On that spring Monday following the weekend when clocks have been nudged up an hour, there's a 7 to 8 percent increase in traffic mishaps. Six months later the reverse happens; on the autumn Monday after clocks are turned back to retrieve the "lost" sixty minutes, the number of crashes decreases at about the same rate.

Daylight come, and we want go sleep. Experts say inattentive, drowsy drivers, getting too few slumber hours, create the annual traffic mayhem.

Daytime

The Bureau of Justice illuminates the statistic that overall violent crime, like robberies, homicides, and assaults, occurs more often during the day than at night.

(See *Afternoons; Between 3 P.M. and 4 P.M.; Mornings; Nighttime*)

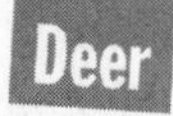

Deer

The proverbial deer in the headlights is creating havoc on U.S. roadways. Every year, the wild animals cause a half a million vehicle accidents, which kill 100 people and injure thousands more. A good 20 million deer roam, not only on the range, but also in food-and-water-plentiful suburbia as the animals' woodland habitat rapidly shrinks. Be on the lookout for the tick-ridden critters (deer are the main carriers of the parasite that causes Lyme disease in humans, which left untreated, can severely damage the heart and nervous system), especially when they're friskiest in the early morning and evening hours, and during the November and December mating season.

(See *Jerky*)

Deli Meats

Your bologna has a problem.

It could be infected with listeria, a stomach-spamming bacteria that contaminates the food supply by passing from water and soil to vegetables and animals. Listeria's no slouch—it kills about 425 people every year.

One of the largest mass listeria outbreaks—so far—happened in 1998, with more than seventy-five confirmed cases and seventeen deaths from tainted deli meats and hot dogs. Millions of meat products were recalled from the market, including chicken burritos sold as airline in-flight meals.

Don't count on the government's protection. Frankly, you're on your own, since Uncle Sam doesn't require manufacturers to screen processed food for microbes. Next time you've got the munchies for a slab of salami or a chili dog, remember that ready-to-eat foods really aren't. Food safety experts say to boil your processed meats first. Yum. People most susceptible to illness—pregnant women, newborns, older folks, and people with weakened immune systems—should veto plates of cold cuts, hot dogs, and soft cheeses.

(See *Brie; Hot Dogs*)

Deodorant

The stench of a woman—and a man—is quelled with a swipe of deodorant or antiperspirant. For that, our B.O.-averse society remains ever-so-grateful, but an ingredient in a good many of the commercial odor eaters is aluminum, a chemical that can cause skin breakouts, and has been found in four times the normal concentration of some Alzheimer's patients' brain cells, which leads some medical experts to suspect the chemical might have a role in causing the debilitating disease.

In preference to smelling bad, teenagers would rather breathe their last. Sadly, an English sixteen-year-old did just that; he died of a heart attack following months of spraying himself with deodorant at least twice a day in his unventilated bedroom. The coroner ruled that the lad was overcome by "excessive use of antiperspirants." The obsessive teen had ten times the lethal dose of propane and butane in his blood, but he must have smelled divine.

Dieting

America is a zaftig nation. More than half the population are roly-polys—either moderately or morbidly overweight. Toting extra pounds has its health hazards, but trying to lose the lard can be dangerous, too.

Here's the skinny. Low-calorie diets can cause wooziness, intolerance to cold, and constipation. Abstain from carbos and the body doesn't eliminate uric acid, which can bring on gout. Cut out all fats—a nutrient-poor diet—and the risk of cancer and heart disease spikes. Extremely low-fat diets tend to increase triglycerides and decrease HDL, the good cholesterol. Dieting may even reduce bone mineral density of the hips and spine, which could boost the risk of fractures and osteoporosis.

Dietitians preach moderation to the corpulent and lean alike, advising to eat a variety of foods, especially fruits and veggies, to drink a lot of water, and, of course, exercise.

Dinner Music

Blame it on the bossa nova. Listening to music while you eat could pack on extra pounds.

Research orchestrated at a Swedish nursing home showed that ditties played during dinner increase the appetite, as well as pacify irritability and alleviate depression. During the study, two weeks of soothing music had the most calming effect on the nursing home residents; a fourteen-day diet of contemporary pop tunes spurred them to scarf more dessert than during serenade-free periods. The staff got into the swing of things, too, dishing out more generous food portions when the music played.

Lesson learned: Refrain from refrains when trying to trim down.

Dirty Mouths

Your mouth is a #%&*^@! cesspool. A good many of the 400 species of bacteria that wallow in your oral cavity are poised to rot your gums, eat away at the underlying bone, and cause your teeth to fall out.

People with crappy teeth and gums are 1.5 to 2 times as likely to suffer a fatal heart attack and nearly 3 times as likely to have a stroke as those without periodontal disease. What gives? Disease-causing bacteria sneak into the bloodstream through inflamed gums to cause tiny artery-clogging blood clots. There's evidence, too, that periodontal disease can worsen cases of diabetes, chronic bronchitis, and emphysema, and that oral infections can induce premature labor.

What are you waiting for? Floss!

Dishwashers

Loaded with danger, dishwashers were responsible for cycling close to 9,000 people through hospital emergency rooms in 1997. The worked-over patients received care for burns they got from heating

elements, for arm and leg lacerations from falling against open doors, and for wounds after reaching inside for skin-puncturing knives and forks.

(See *Washing Dishes*)

Do-It-Yourselfing

Resist the urge to do it yourself. It's a tinker's damn.

Considering the tools of the craft—pliers, drills, screwdrivers, sanders, hammers and nails, heavy-duty staplers—it's hardly surprising that during 1997 close to a quarter of a million handy-capped people were sewn up, put in casts, and treated for burns and other self-inflicted wounds.

(See *Woodworking*)

Doctors' Writing

A nifty sting by Welsh researchers supplied a new but not-so-funny punchline to the timeworn jokes about doctors' illegible handwriting. The crafty investigators persuaded a group of ninety-two doctors, nurses, and administrators to carefully write their names, the alphabet, and the numbers from zero to nine, fibbing to the medicos that their handwriting would help test a new computer software, when actually the samples were going to be evaluated by an optical scanner that picks out unrecognizable characters.

Nurses' and administrators' handwriting fared best. Doctors' scrawled alphabets had almost twice the error rate of the other two groups. All the scribblers did better with numbers; the doctors scored only one error; nurses and administrators, none. The report published in the *British Medical Journal* concludes: "This study suggests that doctors, even when asked to be as neat as possible, produce handwriting that is worse than that of other professions."

Corny jokes aside, it's nothing to chuckle about because sloppy handwriting can create misunderstandings between physicians and patients (and among medical specialists) that could have tragic consequences. According to the FDA, medication errors, such as getting the wrong dose or wrong drug, injure an estimated 1.3 million Americans each year.

(See *Hospitals*)

Dogs

Some best friend. Dogs are responsible for 4.5 million biting injuries every year, and send nearly 334,000 humans to be stitched up in hospital emergency departments.

With a good jaw clamp, Rover can exert hundreds of pounds of crushing pressure, with the human face as favored target (mail carriers get nipped most often in the lower extremities). You're barking up the wrong tree if you think precious Fifi won't sink her French-poodle canines into a neighbor's arm. Pet dogs do most of the biting, close to home, with almost half of all injuries provoked by the bitee; kids, especially little boys, are attacked most often.

Worse than its bite are the gnarly germs on a dog's teeth. *The Journal of the American Medical Association* mutters that cultures from 107 infected dog and cat bites turned up 152 kinds of bacteria, with an average of five kinds of germs per chomp. Eighty-five percent of dog bites harbor potential illness-causing bugs, including those that can cause meningitis and blood infections.

A serious bite injury could lay you up in the hospital as long as four days—that's twenty-eight in dog days.

(See *Cats; Hedgehogs; Lizards; Parakeets*)

Dolphins

Say it ain't so! Dolphins are nothing but warm-blooded killers. Marine scientists have watched, in amazement, as the grinning mammals have bludgeoned to death hundreds of porpoises and have even slaughtered their own offspring. Unlike most animal

killers, dolphins' murderous rampages seem unrelated to the need for food. With growing evidence of the unprovoked oceanic savagery, the National Marine Fisheries Service thinks the wave of so-called therapeutic and spiritual treks by humans who want to frolic among the creatures is a tourist time bomb waiting to explode.

The less adventurous swimmers who float among well-trained dolphins held in captivity are in little danger, say federal officials. It's in the wild where a communal dip with 12-foot-long, sharp-toothed, deliberate killers can be downright perilous. Get a few things straight: Dolphins haven't saved drowning sailors, and they don't enjoy splish-splashing with people or get their jollies from swimming alongside boats. Nor do they protect humans from shark attacks or chatter in dolphinese. They're highly intelligent, ferocious beasts who have already bitten and bumped dozens of swimmers. If you want to sleep with the fishes, dolphins will be more than happy to oblige.

Dominating Conversations

Stifle it. You'll live longer.

Psychologists tell us that men who dominate conversations and constantly interrupt others ("gasbags" is the medical terminology) are more prone to die earlier than their easygoing brethren.

Interviewed over 22 years by shrinks at the University of Kansas, 750 men were scored on behavior characteristics, like verbal competitiveness, loudness, and self-aggrandizement. As reported in the *Journal of the American Psychosomatic Society*, the overbearing buttinskys of the group were about 60 percent more likely to die at an earlier age than were the more deferential fellows, no matter the cause of death.

Doctors suggest that a more easygoing lifestyle could help lower levels of unhealthy stress hormones and might let the rest of us get a word in edgewise.

(See *Assertiveness*)

Doorbells

Ding dong, death calling.

For people with a rare heart rhythm, a sudden sound can make them faint—or even die. This condition is called long QT syndrome, or LQTS, an abnormality of the heart that can provoke an irregular and deadly heartbeat, reports the *Journal of the American College of Cardiology*. People with LQTS, if it's detected early, can be treated with medication.

Doors

Exactly how people injure themselves on doors, door frames, and door sills isn't entirely an open-and-shut case, although an estimated 400,000 manage somehow to do so.

Douching

Bag the douche routine. All that spritzing and spraying is completely unnecessary—the vagina is self-cleaning, after all—and might even do harm to delicate tissue by washing away nature's protective bacteria. Physicians say that frequent douching may raise a woman's chance of developing cervical cancer and could increase the likelihood of contracting Chlamydia infections and bacterial vaginosis. Medical research shows that three-or-more-times-a-month douchers have 3.5 times the risk of developing pelvic inflammatory disease than do once-a-monthers.

Downsizing

You dodged the pink slip—again—but your company's latest downsizing is making you ill. Studies show that workers for companies that had frequent layoffs took twice as many sick days as employees at businesses where only minor axing occurred. The call-in-sick workers weren't goldbrickers; absences longer than three days were doctor certified, reports *The Lancet.*

Drinking Fountains

It's goodnight at the oasis for scores of sippers who knock themselves silly at drinking fountains. It's mostly little squirts who experience painful run-ins with the water spouts; other victims have received electric shocks, second degree burns, and nasty facial lacerations from the damp hazards.

Driving at Night

Traffic death rates are three times greater at night than during the day. Depth perception, color recognition, and peripheral vision are compromised after sundown. Booze, a significant factor in many fatal crashes, makes weekend nights the most lethal of all.

(See *Weekends*)

Driving in New Hampshire

New Hampshire might consider changing its state motto from "Live Free *or* Die" to "Live Free *and* Die." National Transportation Safety Board statistics prove what anyone with a brain knows: Seat belts save lives. Still, New Hampshire remains the only state in the union that stubbornly refuses to make them law for vehicle occupants over eighteen years of age. Its nickname, the Granite State, seems most appropriate.

Driving Music

Do we care that the jerks who drive cars with jet-take-off-decibel-level stereo systems are damaging the best ears of their life? Of course not. But the trunks of funk with the superamped, concrete-rattling noise are road hazards that we all have to worry about. The bah-boom, bah-booms interfere with the obnoxious drivers' ability to notice objects coming at them, like darting-into-the-street children, emergency vehicles, or other cars.

University of Sydney researchers monitored the reaction times of drivers seated in front of computer monitors were equipped with steering wheels and gas and brake pedals. During simulation drives, the test subjects listened to music played at a relatively low 55-decibel level, or to tunes boosted up to 85 decibels, or they drove in silence.

The results were inharmonious. The Australians conclude that when music is played at any decibel level, drivers aren't able to effectively scan the environment. When car stereos are cranked to full volume, drivers' reaction times to peripheral objects are slowed down a tenth of a second, which may not seem like much, but it could mean boom and doom for that darting child.

Drowsy Truckers

King of the road needs a nap. Truckers only sleep, on average, a little more than 4.5 hours a day, which is a problem for everyone on the road since the leading cause of big-truck accidents is driver fatigue. Truckers on the nod are as menacing as drunk drivers on the highway, claims the Stanford University Sleep Research Center.

Drowsy driving is perilous, no matter what kind of vehicle is being handled. Sounding a wake-up call, the U.S. National Highway Traffic Safety Administration estimates that 100,000 crashes a year involve fatigue. The likelihood of smash-ups increases with the number of hours behind the wheel and during the hours between midnight and 6 A.M.—sort of a trucker's job description. Big rig drivers are susceptible to fatigue-related crashes since they usually drive more miles, and are on the road when the body's natural rhythm craves sleep. The Sleep Foundation says that truck drivers may have a higher prevalence of sleep apnea, a

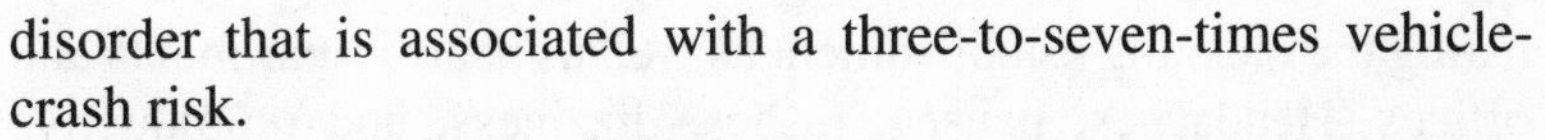

disorder that is associated with a three-to-seven-times vehicle-crash risk.

When truckers drive sleepy, others get hurt. In fatal passenger car/truck crashes, 98 percent of the deaths occur to the people in the passenger vehicles. In 1997, large trucks accounted for 3 percent of registered vehicles but were involved in 12 percent of all passenger vehicle occupant deaths and in 22 percent of multiple-vehicle passenger vehicle occupant deaths.

Drumsticks

Chickens are foul. About 20 percent of all U.S.-raised birds are infected with the harmful salmonella bacteria, and many more (some studies estimate up to 90 percent) are contaminated with the gut-churning, antibiotic-resisting campylobacter bacteria.

And, how's this for a cluck-up: The Department of Agriculture says it's okay for poultry processors to sell chicken that's been tainted with excrement. Excrement! The doodoo boo-boo happens when processing machines accidentally puncture digestive tracts when scooping out internal organs. Oops. Don't bother tossing out the feces-riddled meat, squawks the USDA to chicken processors; just spray the dirty bird with chlorinated water and it can go to market. In 1994, the very same federal agency tested chickens from major poultry producers and discovered that 88 percent were contaminated with fecal bacteria. Gad.

Go farm-raised on this one.

Dry-cleaned Clothes

Dressed to kill.

Some dry cleaners use a highly toxic chemical suspected of causing cancer. More than 200 million pounds of perchloroethylene, used annually by 35,000 dry cleaners across North America, whisks away gravy stains but also enters the atmosphere, contaminating the cleaning establishment as well as nearby apartments and offices. Headaches, nausea, rashes, dizziness, and reproductive and memory problems have been associated with the cleaning solvent. Greenpeace, the hard-core environmental group, fumes that several studies have indicated that perc exposure increases the jeopardy of acquiring esophagus, lung, kidney, and liver cancers, and that water contaminated with the chemical has been linked to cases of leukemia and pancreatic, bladder, and cervical cancers.

Small amounts of perc, known also to attack the central nervous system, are released into the air by freshly cleaned clothes; the residue can cause throat, eye, and nose irritations. The maximum safe level of perc is 100 parts per million; one study measured 350 parts per million inside a car 15 minutes after dry-cleaned clothes had been placed inside.

Clean green with a dry cleaner that uses water and special non-toxic soaps.

E

Ear Candling

Ear candling, the so-called remedy for earwax buildup, is insane. The process: Insert a wax-soaked, cone-shaped piece of cloth in the ear canal; next, light it. As it burns, proponents (and there are actually some out there) say it creates a vacuum that sucks out the earwax, but the gunk that appears on the cloth is nothing more than wick ashes and wax from the cone. It's not safe, cautions the stalwart FDA, which considers the ear candle an unregulated medical device.

Write this down: Hot wax burns. Physicians who treat the ear candled for blistered ears as well as ear canal obstructions and infections and perforated eardrums say get real—ear candling is bunk. Snuff it.

Earlobe Creases

It's a new wrinkle to worry about. Creased earlobes could be fairly good indicators of cardiac problems.

Doctors at the University of Chicago, speculating that the diagonal creases are the result of blood vessel changes like those that cause heart disease, found that the creased-lobed are eight times more inclined to have heart disease and are much more apt to die from cardiac problems than those without the furrow.

Earplugs

America's turning a deaf ear. Way ahead of one of the most unpleasant ravages of Father Time, nearly 15 percent of youngsters ages six to nineteen, and 17 percent of adults eighteen to forty-four, already show signs of hearing loss. Blame it on everyday toxic noise—the unrelenting bombardment of workplace racket, high-amped music venues and stereo systems, gas-chugging lawnmowers, screaming sirens, noisy appliances, and louder-than-an-ambulance-siren toys.

Since the world's not likely to ratchet down, you need to wise up. Wear earplugs, but be gentle; the chestnut about not putting anything in your ear smaller than your elbow holds true. Shoved too far down your ear canal, the hard plastic or soft pliable noise buffers can get wedged, needing a doctor's skill to retrieve them.

(See *Chain Saws; Movie Previews; Rock Concerts; Women in Labor; Woodworking; Yard Work*)

Eating Out

Out-to-eat spending has increased about 340 percent since the mid-seventies, a nice *ca-ching* for the restaurant biz but it's not doing much for weight watchers. *The Journal of the American Dietetic Association* reports that women who frequently dine out

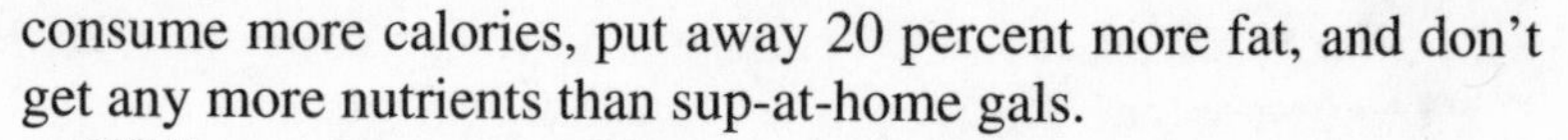

consume more calories, put away 20 percent more fat, and don't get any more nutrients than sup-at-home gals.

While you're out gorging on calories, request the *No Breathing* section. The indoor air of some nonsmoking restaurants isn't as virginal as you think. Kitchen pollution, cooking-fume gunk, exposes patrons to harmful levels of airborne particles that can promote or exacerbate a menu of respiratory problems.

Educations

Soap and education are not as sudden as a massacre but they are more lethal in the long run.—Mark Twain

Schooling can make you smart. The more you know, the more you hurt.

The upshot of a large-scale, first-of-its-kind research project is that people with higher levels of education are more susceptible to getting tension headaches. Of the more than 13,000 people in the study, the ones with graduate degrees endured the dull, squeezing head pain more often than high school dropouts.

Women aged thirty-something were most inclined to have tension headaches (no doubt from slamming against that damn glass ceiling). Although the exact cause of tension headaches is still unknown, the researchers speculate that they're triggered by stress, certain foods, and sleep-pattern changes, and are exacerbated by deadline-driven, high-stress jobs and by family-life demands of the highly educated.

Egg Cartons

The dirty dozen. Cradling eggs from farm to market to fridge, polystyrene packages can contaminate their delicate cargo. Volatile chemicals have seeped from the plastic containers and migrated through the porous shells of eggs into the edible parts. No yolk. The Louisiana Agricultural Experiment Station reports that dishes cooked with eggs that had been stored in polystyrene containers for two weeks registered seven times more ethylbenzene and styrene in them than those prepared from fresh uncartoned farm eggs.

(See *Eggs*)

Eggnog

The proof is in the punch, but no matter how much liquor spikes the eggnog, if salmonella-infected eggs are in the mix, it won't kill the puky bacteria, and you could find yourself spending the holidays ho-ho-hoing over the john.

(See *Egg Cartons; Eggs*)

Eggs

They've taken a beating, but it boils down to this: Eating eggs can be a sickening experience. The Centers for Disease Control and Prevention clucks over the fact that 2.3 million of the 46.8 billion eggs produced every year in the United States are infected with the smarmy salmonella bacteria. The USDA estimates that 900,000 people fall ill each year from contaminated eggs, a much too low calculation, laments the Center for Science in the Public Interest, which puts the number at a whopping 4 million.

Keep your sunnyside up but don't order them. Have your eggs fully cooked, not raw, soft-boiled, or poached.

(See *Egg Cartons; Eggnog*)

Electrolysis

Don't try this at home. Licensed electrolysists know how and where on your hirsute body to poke a root-destroying needle, and can judge the precise amount of voltage to apply. Jab yourself and you're liable to be walking on infected, as well as hairy, legs.

Elevators

Odds are you'll never get shafted, but not so lucky are the elevator riders who do get bruised and battered after trip-ups and fall-downs, who suffer amputated arms, legs, fingers, and toes from out-of-control cars or from door-closing glitches. Some reported accidents have been truly gruesome limb manglers, including a 1995 decapitation in a New York City runaway elevator. In 1998, the ABC television program "20/20" noted that more than 100 deaths have occurred from elevator mishaps since 1991.

Unfortunately, federal regulations regarding safety oversight aren't on the books, and a hodgepodge of state and local government agencies and private firms with no mandate to compile national accident statistics, have been handed the enormous task of inspecting and enforcing building codes for the 660,000 elevators in the United States. Some safety experts make the claim that the number of maimed riders, estimated to be 10,000 each year, is more likely somewhere between 18,000 and 27,000.

Exercise caution: Take the stairs.

(See *Banisters; Escalators*)

Empty Day Books

Over the years, gobs of data have linked social isolation to illness and death, with various studies all proving that not having close personal ties can weaken health and decrease longevity. People with few social networks are about four times more likely to get sick than those with six or more types of connecting relationships. Healthy, but unfriended men and women are twice as likely to die over a period of a decade or so as are robust, less monastic people. Live-alone heart attack survivors die at twice the rate of those who live with others, and people with heart disease have a poorer chance of survival if they're unmarried. Women who feel alienated from social interactions die of breast and ovarian cancer at 3.5 times the expected rate; advanced

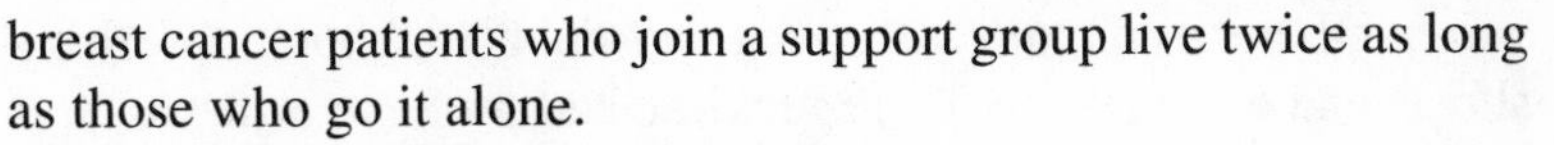

breast cancer patients who join a support group live twice as long as those who go it alone.

Connect the dots. Make a friend.

(See *Friends and Relations*)

Escalators

Every year, some 5,500 escalator riders are treated in hospital emergency rooms, with falls accounting for 75 percent of mishaps, entrapment of feet, hands, and shoes about 20 percent. Most of the moving violations (some causing permanent disfigurements or disabilities) are blamed on worn or faulty equipment.

The American Academy of Pediatrics, reading the riot act about children being at great risk for sustaining horrific injuries, cite studies that prove kids are more likely to be trapped when they glide rather than step off the end of the escalator.

Riders of all ages should stand in the middle of the escalator, hold the handrail, and pull up loose shoelaces and dangling scarves, drawstrings, and mittens that are easily gobbled by moving parts. Use the elevator when toting strollers, walkers, or carts. Plan ahead: Know where to find the emergency shutoff button.

(See *Elevators*)

Expensive Athletic Shoes

Wearing pricey athletic shoes causes a greater number of more injuries—123 percent more—than sporting a pair of cheap ones, says a biomechanics and internal medicine specialist. In the *British Journal of Sports Medicine*, Dr. Steven Robbins of Canada's McGill University recommends slipping on an ordinary pair of $40 athletic shoes instead of a $140 brand-name pair.

Dr. Robbins doesn't fault big-ticket shoes for causing sports injuries, but rather heaps blame on advertising hoopla for creating a false sense of security in shoe wearers, who are duped by the safety claims of the air-cushioned, gel-bubbled, shock-absorbing shoes, and are therefore more reckless and prone to injury than if they'd tread lighter in cheaper footwear.

To validate his thesis, the doctor rigged an experiment to measure the impact of repeated footfalls on different types of surfaces. He had fifteen shoeless males step on to platforms. One was bare (the platform, not the test subject), the others were covered with the same shoe sole material, the kind used to make expensive sneakers. Before the test, the men listened to an advertising pitch about each platform covering. One covering was hyped as providing superior impact absorption, another was touted as a new product with an unknown safety potential, while the bare platform was given a poor-impact absorption review of having a reputation for a high risk for injury.

The platform advertised as having the most injury protection had an 11 percent higher impact measurement than did the bare platform. The volunteers, when landing on what they thought was cheap material, tended to protect themselves from injury by not making such a hard impact.

Run, don't walk, to the discount store.

(See *Shoes*)

Eyeglasses

Injury statistics for eyewear are out-of-sight. In 1997, hospital emergency rooms treated an estimated 12,700 four-eyed patients for, among other things, facial bruises and lacerations, corneal abrasions and cheek punctures caused by eyeglasses. See to it you're more circumspect with your specs.

(See *Contact Lenses*)

Fallen Leaves

After a rain, streets cluttered with dead leaves can become perilously slick. Drive with care.

(See *Autumn*)

Fashion Magazines

Fashion is a form of ugliness so intolerable that we have to alter it every six months.—Oscar Wilde

The look is wearing thin, especially for young girls, who are devout readers of fashion magazines that flaunt gossamer-thin models as the ideal body image. The adolescent zine readers tend to dislike their own shapes, and view themselves as overweight and unappealing to the opposite sex. More than two-thirds of girls in grades five through twelve admitted to Boston researchers that magazine photos of whippet-legged models influenced them to diet or to exercise to lose weight, when only 29 percent of the 548 adolescents interviewed were overweight.

Displays of size-2 models weigh heavy on the average teen girls' self-image, and according to the endeavor by the Harvard Medical School and Harvard School of Public Health, the fashion layouts could be a factor in some young girls developing serious eating disorders, like bulimia and anorexia nervosa, as the youngsters try to attain unhealthy body weights. "Our message is that these magazines have a very large impact on young girls," says epidemiologist Dr. Alison E. Field, the study's lead author. "If the images in these magazines are unhealthy, that's a problem."

Fat Necks

Chin up. Men tend to carry a greater proportion of flab around their necks than do women, which might be why they suffer more often from a common but truly dangerous disorder. No, not Tight Collar Syndrome, but sleep apnea, Greek for "without breath." People with the condition snort and gurgle while asleep, and literally stop breathing, sometimes hundreds of times during the night, when the extra tissue at the back of the throat sags and narrows the air passageway. People with sleep apnea have much higher rates of hypertension, heart irregularities, stroke, and premature death than do people without the ailment.

(See *Chubby Cheeks; Long Faces; Snoring*)

Faucets

The news has leaked that faucets—chrome playgrounds teeming with salmonella and *E. coli*—are one of the ickiest things in the house. Good hand-washing techniques, plus an occasional swipe with bleach on the spigots, will take care of the bugaboos, but you're still not home free.

The whole bathroom scene is ground zero for disaster, responsible for sending thousands of lacerated, bruised, and burned people to emergency rooms. Every year more than 200,000 reported injuries are from hot-water burns alone, and the number of bathtub falls trails close behind.

(See *Toilets*)

Fire Engines

Those in the color biz say that in the dark, our eyes have difficulty seeing red, and after adapting to bright light, can only make out the color poorly. An article published in the *Journal of Safety Research* shows that the frequency of intersection accidents involving red fire engines is twice that of lime yellow ones, and yet there's been no great hue and cry to change the traditional look of all pumpers. The National Fire Protection Association reports almost 15,000 accidents involving fire emergency vehicles in 1997, but has no comparative data regarding vehicle color. Even so, it seems wise to get the hook and ladder and a bucket of paint.

Firing Someone

"Before you clear out your desk, mind calling 911?"

Giving an employee the ax could mean your own termination. It's a given, with tons of corroborating research, that workplace stress increases the peril of heart disease, but researchers at Beth Israel–Deaconess Medical Center in Boston wanted to find out if specific, brief events could be linked to heart attacks, so they asked almost 800 cardiac patients what kind of work week they'd had before suffering their heart attacks. The analysis clearly shows that while being laid off, or quitting a job, or being promoted slightly raises the probability of having a heart attack, having to sack someone doubles the risk.

First Week of the Month

The first week of the month is a doozy. During those seven days, combined death rates from accidents, suicides, homicides, and substance abuse related deaths typically jump 14 percent when compared with the last week of the previous month, according to a investigation published in *The New England Journal of Medicine*. Deaths caused by cancer, heart, liver, and respiratory problems are also higher—about 1 percent so.

Analyzing nearly 32 million death certificates, researchers discovered that the disparities among the weekly death rates were even higher among the poor and suggested that the morbid trend may be caused by the availability of discretionary funds, which some people use to purchase drugs and alcohol when benefit checks arrive at the beginning of the month.

Fish Tanks

There is something about a home aquarium which sets my teeth on edge the moment I see it. Why anyone would want to live with a small container of stagnant water populated by a half-dead guppy is beyond me.
—S. J. Perelman

Troll the *Journal of Accident and Emergency Medicine* to learn about the dangers of cleaning fish tanks. An immersed hand with even the tiniest cut or abrasion can become infected with a brutish bacteria that commonly thrives in home aquariums. Doctors call the bacterial skin disease "fish tank granuloma," and usually prescribe a two-to-four-month antibiotic regimen to cast away infection.

If you're angling to prevent the stubborn rash and swelling, a pair of long rubber gloves will do the trick.

Fishing

The sport lures. But the dangers of fishing have been codified.

Overuse injuries are common among fly fishers. The repetitive motion of cocking the arm back, snapping the wrist, and reeling in the line can aggravate tendons and cause carpal tunnel syndrome, the painful repetitive stress malady commonly suffered by assembly-line workers and keyboard peckers.

Freshwater fishing harbors another potential peril—this one from a lake-water-lurking organism called *A.hydrophila.* Trivial injuries, such as snagging a finger on a fishhook, if not cleaned properly (*not* with lake water), can lead to a serious, tissue-killing infection, like gangrene, and eventually limb amputation. Go fish, but pack an antiseptic in your tackle box.

(See *Lakes*)

Five Servings a Day

Nutritionists on Uncle Sam's payroll rag Americans to eat five daily servings of fruit and vegetables. Strange, though, how the official admonition leaves out the salient fact that as shipments of imported produce have doubled over the past years, so have produce-related illnesses.

Your grocery store probably stocks produce from at least ninety countries; in the winter, 60 percent of our food comes from foreign shores. Viva la culinary difference, but recently, Americans have suffered from high-profile outbreaks of produce-borne illnesses, like cyclosporiasis from Guatemalan raspberries, a vicious strain of *E. coli* 0157:H7 linked to Mexican lettuce, hepatitis A carried by tainted south-of-the-border strawberries, and salmonella poisoning from Netherlands-grown alfalfa sprouts. An infection route is hard to pin down; it could start in contaminated soil and water or in a supermarket's dirty veggie bins.

The government, with its crazy quilt of regulations, isn't much help. As the understaffed, woefully underfunded principal food-inspection agency, the FDA looks only at about 0.2 percent (an iffy number at best) of all imported food for pesticides and pathogens and has no authority to peek at foreign food facilities or growing fields. Even more worrisome is the charge by critics who claim that the government agency is ignoring the worst-of-the-worst bugs, like new, lethal strains of *E. coli*, parasitic ailments, and emerging diseases from developing countries.

One inquiry rooted out that imported food is three times more likely to contain illegal pesticide residues than is homegrown food. Labels won't do much good since growers and shippers can relabel or rebox foreign-grown produce. Grow your own or buy organic or shop locally from farmers' markets—wherever, wash the heck out of all your produce before eating those five servings.

(See *Alfalfa Sprouts; Baked Potatoes; Parsley; Produce Sections*)

Fizzy Drinks

Hold the bubbly. The effervescent *New England Journal of Medicine* reports of a rare disorder—deglutition syncope—that causes people to faint when they swallow, and which can be provoked by ice-cold, fizzy drinks. The chilly carbonation sets off heart rate slowdowns and a quick plummet in blood pressure, culminating in dizzy spells or fainting.

Flaming Drinks

Let's try "Potent Potables" for $100, Alex.

Stay out of jeopardy; never order flaming drinks. Concocted with high-octane alcohol and set ablaze with a match strike, the liquor can have a flame-thrower effect when more hooch is poured from the bottle into the fiery glass. Flames can shimmy up the stream of alcohol, flashing a whoosh of fire out of the bottle's neck in a heated rush.

The American Surgeon reports three cases of severe burns from firewater; each high-octane drinker required skin grafts leaving them with permanent facial scars. Hotshot, fireproof your highball: drinking and striking don't mix.

Florida

When the shark bites, his jaws are likely to be munching on a swimmer somewhere off the Florida coast. Of the twenty-five attacks that occurred in North American waters in 1998, nineteen were in the Sunshine State (aptly named since it boasts the highest incidence per capita of the deadly skin cancer melanoma).

Scratch swimming in Florida's lakes or ponds, too. Gators, at least a million of them, prowl inland waterways, golf courses, and back yards in search of mates and food (not necessarily the same) since the state's commercial and residential developments have gobbled up the primordial creatures' natural habitats.

Man eaters or no, Florida's waters are safer than its streets, the country's deadliest avenues for pedestrians. Three of the top five ped killers are Florida cities: Orlando, Tampa–St. Petersburg, and

Miami–Fort Lauderdale. Won't do any good to hop on a bike, since the state claims the nation's highest death rate for bicyclists. Sheesh.

(See *Alligator Shoes*)

Flower Shows

The bloom's definitely off. The rare but deadly Legionnaire's bacteria that lurked among the posies at a 1998 Netherlands flower show killed seventeen petalphiles and infected hundreds more. The outbreak was blamed on disease-spritzing fountains located throughout the exhibit space.

Football Games

Quarterbacks aren't the only ones reciting Hail Marys. Football-game spectators pray they don't end up on injured lists. Roughly one out of 1,000 fans needed medical attention at the University of South Carolina's seven home games in 1995. Half of the grandstanders complained of headaches, nearly one out of five had some sort of injury, and one in ten groused about digestive problems—probably too much pigskin.

(See *Bowl Games; Cheerleading*)

French Fries

Hooray! Americans are eating 20 percent more vegetables today than twenty-five years ago. Um, hold the applause. Greasy, salty french fries make up about a quarter of the servings. Oh well.

An especially fatty meal, like a juicy burger and a side order of french fries, could bring on a heart attack in someone with coronary heart disease, since dietary fat entering the bloodstream may cause blood clot formation.

(See *Baked Potatoes; Five Servings a Day*)

Frequent Flying

In 1998, 614 million commercial air passengers took to the sky, a friendly one at that. Zero fatal accidents were reported, but the number of bad air days was hardly peanuts. By one count—the Air Transport Association's—each year, there are more than 10,000 medical in-flight incidences on the nine largest U.S. airlines (responsible for 65 percent of all passengers flown by American carriers), which is more than twenty-eight emergencies a day—far higher than the FAA's 1991 estimate of two to three per day.

The in-flight death rate—an estimated 350 passengers die each year on board American planes—has soared since 1988. Officials at Kennedy Airport in New York admit they remove dead bodies from inbound flights between five and ten times a year. More passengers on long-haul flights, a greater number of elderly fliers, overexertion from carrying heavy baggage, and the excitement of travel have all been blamed for the higher death rate.

The biggest medical complaints: nausea from motion sickness and eating airline food; heart attacks (the leading cause of death during air travel); chest pains; back miseries—from sitting for long hours and from carrying hefty luggage; head injuries caused by falling items from overstuffed luggage bins; food-borne diseases; earaches; and dehydration.

Sardine-packed passengers are primed to suffer from deep vein thrombosis, or "economy-class syndrome." Sitting for long periods—four hours or more—in dry-air cabins reduces circulation in the legs by 50 percent and can summon blood clots to form in the lower extremities; if a piece of the clot breaks off and makes its way to the lungs, it can be deadly. Passenger legroom is only getting scarcer as some airlines remodel first-class sections at the expense and comfort of steerage class. What to do? During a long flight, walk the aisles, lift and lower your legs, drink plenty of water (be sure and ask for bottled water since the water on planes comes from the point of origin where taste and safety standards may not be to your liking).

Germs fly free. Infectious diseases, like colds and tuberculosis, spread through planes' recirculated air, already full of toxins like carbon dioxide and residual gases from chemical solutions used to clean the aircraft. Experts have found *E. coli* bacteria and other bugs that cause diseases—everything from rashes to fatal encephalitis—contaminating bathroom door handles, toilet seats, and sinks. Since passengers—in seats designed more for a supermodel's derrière than middle-American tushes—are squeezed in kennel-close quarters, germs can spread quickly and efficiently.

It's called "cabin fever," or "mile-high madness." And, madness it is. Flight attendants get punched, ticket agents pummeled, drunken passengers defecate on food carts. Assaults on crew members rose 5 percent from 1995 to 1996, and the Association of Flight Attendants regrets that the trend shows no signs of waning. At least one-quarter of all crew interference incidents are alcohol related, according to the Air Transport Association, and the International Crew Association reports that the number of violent confrontations, which endanger the lives of everyone on board an airplane, has quadrupled since 1995.

(See *Airplane Aisle Seats; Bottled Water*)

Fridays

TGIF? No, TGFI: Thank God For Insurance.

More car accidents happen on Fridays than on any other day of the week. The fender benders peak during the day's morning and afternoon rush hours.

(See *Mondays; Saturdays; Weekends*)

Friends and Relations

Are you the kind of person who never meets a stranger? Try it.

Most victims of violent crimes know their assailant. More than 70 percent of all rapes and sexual assaults are committed by people well-known to the victim, and almost half of murder victims are related to or acquainted with their killers, squeals the Bureau of Justice.

(See *Empty Day Books; Sweethearts*)

Frosted Eye Shadow

Go to the matte on this one. The American Academy of Ophthalmology advises against wearing pearlized eye shadow. The iridescent ground oyster shells or tinsel can scratch your eyeballs, especially if a glittery particle burrows under a contact lens.

Frozen Beef Patties

It's not mad cow disease, but when the venerable *British Medical Journal* discusses frozen beef patties, there must be something to worry about. There is. It's the hazard of using a sharp knife to pry the ice-chilled slabs of meat apart that prompted physicians to write about "beefburger" slashes, some severe enough to warrant emergency surgery. The English doctors also warned of the perils of slicing apart frozen sausages but not a whisper about crumpets.

(See *Bagels*)

Furnaces

In the heat of the night, and day, carbon monoxide from faulty furnaces, gas ranges, and water heaters kills some 200 Americans and sends another 10,000 gasping to emergency rooms each year. Breathing even small amounts of the gas can lead to lasting brain damage. Don't fool around. Hire a technician to check out the furnace every single year, and invest in a carbon monoxide detector, as well as a smoke detector.

G

Gemstones

To the four Cs of gemstone appraisal—carat, clarity, color, cut—add one more: counter, as in Geiger.

In some laboratories, radiation is used to deepen the color of gemstones, greatly increasing their value. Bombarding a $1,200 yellow cats's-eye with radioactive electrons and neutrons produces a dazzling honey-colored gem easily worth $5,000. By the same process, a drab pink tourmaline becomes a brilliant rose-colored sparkler that sells at a premium, and an inferior, light-blue topaz ripens to a dark blue (and expensive) luster.

The stones are radiant, all right, but that's the problem. Nuked gems should be kept in lead casings for several years while their radiation levels taper off. But unscrupulous traders have marketed "hot" cat's-eyes, some registering fifty-one times the U.S. radiation limit. Experts in Bangkok, the world center of gem trading, suspect that thousands of radioactive stones are in circulation in the United States, Asia, and Europe.

George Costanza

George Costanza, the character played by actor Jason Alexander on *Seinfeld,* is responsible for what doctors call the Seinfeld Syncope. As reported in the ever-popular journal *Catheterization and Cardiovascular Diagnosis*, some viewers have fainted, quite literally, with laughter at Costanza's nebbish behavior. They passed out because their chuckling pushed the chest wall on the heart and stopped the flow of blood to the brain. One of George's fans keeled over into his plate of linguine and was rushed to the hospital. Surgical insertion of an inflatable balloon into his arteries helped blood circulate to his brain, allowing the jolly fellow to enjoy Costanza's antics without swooning.

No word yet on bizarre responses to the sitcom's other characters or to what effect, if any, Seinfeld Syncope has on the show's syndication ratings.

Ginseng Extract

Ardent proponents of ginseng claim that the root extract boosts energy and rejuvenates sagging spirits. The truth is, that in some forms, it can even be billed *as* spirits.

Ginseng extract sold in glass vials has been found to contain alcohol—as a teacher in upstate New York discovered when she served the tonic to her fifth grade nutrition class. After sampling the liquid ginseng donated by the local health food store, the students dozed off at their desks. News of the tipsy kids reached the Bureau of Alcohol, Tobacco and Firearms, which subsequently tested fifty-five different ginseng products. Only seven contained pure extract, while the majority was tainted, some with up to 34 percent alcohol—a regular belter when you consider that all beverages exceeding 0.5 percent alcohol must be labeled as booze.

Glasgow

Something's way out of kilter in Scotland. The largest international study of coronary disease finds that Glasgow is the world's heart attack capital. The ten-year project, involving twenty-one countries covering four continents, blames Glasgow's dubious distinction on high levels of smoking among the city's men and women, and on the residents' less-than-heart-healthy eating habits.

Glue Guns

Glue guns are much too easy to come by. This is not a good thing. With no mandatory waiting periods and no background checks, the weapons of crass construction give overdecorators license to overkill. Sequins, glitter, and fringe affixed to furniture, clothing, picture frames—is there no stopping the gun slingers? Maybe a trip to the hospital, where scores of squirters are ministered to for blisters and burns.

Goalposts

Soccer moms should use their heads to prevent kids from fooling around goalposts. At least twenty-seven falling-goalpost injuries, eighteen of which were fatal, have been investigated by the Consumer Product Safety Commission. The average age of the incapacitated children was ten years; they were hurt after climbing on, swinging from, or lifting metal goalposts, or by causing the heavy posts to topple over.

Goggles

Too-tight swim goggles, causing temporary swelling and possibly double vision, can be real eyesores. For all your water sports, get a well-fitting, plump-cushioned pair.

Golf

Golf is a good walk spoiled.—Mark Twain

Golf may not be a contact sport, but fore play is rough. Swinging and twisting, bending and kneeling are par for the course, but even touring pros sustain, on average, two injuries a year, usually from long, joint-punishing sessions on the practice tee. Amateurs fare worse; about 64 percent are indisposed every year, most afflicted with wrenched backs, shoulders, elbows, and wrists. Some players even kink their joints before the first tee by jerking a heavy golf bag out of a car trunk.

Duffers, playing in the sun for hours at a time, are at high risk for skin cancer, and, for the same reason, are prone to heat stroke and dehydration. Threatening weather converts golf clubs, umbrellas, and carts into life-threatening lightning rods. And those clothes! A polyester parade with too many horizontal stripes (and what's up with those knickers?). Besides, an off-balance swing can make the fashion-challenged shirts cause a painful skin chafing—so common it's nicknamed "golfer's nipple."

Don't lick your balls. It's a curious practice by some players who pop golf balls in their mouths for a good tongue cleaning. Convenient way to remove putt-interfering debris, but think about it. Golf courses are sprayed with a myriad of chemicals, including potent pesticides and insecticides, which have given mouth washers serious liver ailments.

Leave the cart at the clubhouse; walking is good exercise, and there's another good reason to hoof it. The Consumer Product Safety Commission has kept score of more than 7,200 injuries and 25 deaths from the buggies.

Gospel Concerts

Hallelujah and pass the oxygen mask.

Gospel/Christian music concerts have the highest likelihood of medical emergencies, sing the brothers and sisters at the journal, *Academic Emergency Medicine,* humming results from a scrutiny of first-aid stations at 405 musical venues, ranging from classical to grunge.

(See *Classical Performances; Rock Concerts*)

Grapefruit Juice

Grapefruit juice doesn't just make the medicine go down—it can turn a normal measure of medicine into pulp friction.

A compound in grapefruit blocks the vital work of liver enzymes that are supposed to break down certain drugs in the body, keeping the dose at a level that the doctor prescribes. Swallowed with the citrus juice, more of a drug is absorbed, which boosts its strength, sometimes to overdose levels, and can even set off abnormal, and sometimes fatal, heart rhythms.

The FDA warns not to quaff grapefruit juice to wash down prescription or over-the-counter antihistamines, as well as some antidepressants, sleeping pills, estrogens, and heart medications.

The effects of grapefruit juice vary from person to person, drug to drug. Ask a doctor or pharmacist about your breakfast squeeze.

(See *Apple Juice; Juice Bars*)

Gray Beards

Only Gramps knows for sure.

Some physicians are concerned that the chemical formulations of hair dyes used to tint graying beards might harm infants and young children who touch and suck the aging-not-very-gracefully faces of their loved ones.

(See *Hugging Daddy*)

Guacamole

Some packaged guacamole contains sulfites that preserve its hey-this-tastes-just-like-cardboard flavor. In some people, sulfites may cause mild to fatal allergic reactions.

Don't be a dip. Make guacamole with fresh avocados.

Guardrails

Taking the high road might not be so wise after all.

Guardrails are supposed to absorb crashes, and to protect vehicles from veering off into other lanes or from careening off tall bridges. The roadway sentinels were designed thirty years ago, before the streets were choked with SUVs, light trucks, and minivans, which sit so high off the ground that guardrails may actually snag the road hogs' wheels, causing the elevated vehicles to roll over on impact. Concerned about potential dangers, the Federal Highway Administration is funding research into improved guardrail systems.

Hairbrushes

Comb through hospitals' injury reports to find the root of hairbrush hazards. Groomers arrive at E.R.s by the hundreds every year suffering from what must be one heckuva beauty regimen. Doctors treat scratched-up eyeballs and punctured mouths, out-of-whack necks, and even dislocated shoulders all attributed to hairbrushing. Go ahead, bristle, but easy on the tangles.

Hair Conditioners

Taming your mane isn't as safe as you think. Hair conditioners with PH—protein hydrolysates like collagen, keratin, elastin, wheat, and almonds—can cause allergic rashes and swollen lips.

Hair Gel

A little dab will do you in, say teachers at an English school, who banned students from wearing chemical hair products, claiming the greasy kid stuff is a fire hazard. A few years back, a gel-coifed boy burned his hair in science class, but pomade manufacturers insist the product is only for grooming, not booming.

Halloween

No use disguising it. Eye-scratching, vision-obstructing masks; kid-tripping costumes; finger-slicing pumpkin carving knives; and clothing-igniting candles make Halloween a very spooky holiday indeed.

Children are four times as likely to be fatally injured by a car on Halloween night than on any other evening. Brake for gremlins.

(See *Pumpkin Carving*)

Halogen Floor Lamps

Reaching curtain-igniting temperatures of 1,200° F, halogen floor lamps are flagrant fire hazards. Forty million of the inexpensive (as cheap as 20 bucks), open-top lamps blaze in houses, hotels, college dorms, and offices. Lamps that were manufactured for the U.S. market after the 1977 Consumer Product Safety Commission requirement of having a bulb shield or a heat-sensitive cut-off switch may be safer, but many lamp owners, like college officials at Vassar and Yale, have banished them from the decor because the torchieres are unsteady, too easily knocked over, which could shatter hot glass fragments across a room.

Hundreds of fires and at least fifteen deaths have been attributed to the lamps. Jazz great Lionel Hampton lost irreplaceable possessions in his Manhattan apartment, gutted when a high-intensity, high-heat halogen floor lamp tipped onto his bed, catching bed clothes on fire. Although Hampton escaped uninjured, twenty-three other people in the building suffered from smoke inhalation.

See the light. Put halogen floor lamps out—on the junk heap.

(See *Yard Sales*)

Handlebars

Helmets and body pads make for safer bike rides, but every year 35,000 children are worked over by handlebars. Kids don't have the upper body strength to push off and away from a bike during a wipe out. Instead, they pitch forward onto the metal handlebars, lacerating spleens, livers, and kidneys.

Safe Moves, a bicycle safety education program, offers tips for safer bike rides: lower the seat so the center of gravity isn't over the handlebars, teach kids to sit back on the seat and how to fall away from the bike, and keep pads on the handlebar grips to cover sharp steel ends.

Hangovers

"There is no cure for the hangover, save death." Robert Benchley's sousy quip is close to what Finnish doctors say happens to drinkers who get hammered too often. Studies show that men who admit having at least one hangover a month have more than a twofold risk of cardiovascular death when compared with men who suffer fewer mornings after.

Hedgehogs

Cranky-dispositioned hedgehogs have replaced the homely potbellied pig as house pet *du jour*. The sharp-quilled, nocturnal animals prefer a quiet environment, are easily frightened by loud noises, bite under stress, and emit a mild toxic irritant from their projecting spines.

(See *Cats; Dogs; Lizards; Parakeets*)

Heimlich Maneuver

The universal sign for choking is not, contrary to popular belief, the N.Y. Mets logo. Rather, it's placing both hands on the throat to signal you can't breathe, which should alert a dinner companion to spring into action, grab you from behind, and give a few quick upper thrusts to the middle of your stomach, forcing the windpipe-clogging food up and out. You'll want to die of embarrassment but you'll live to enjoy dessert.

The Heimlich Maneuver, started too soon, could push the lodged food into a breath-blocking position. If a choker is coughing, it stands to reason he's breathing, so don't assume the Heimlich position right off; let him hack away and the offending morsel might be expelled without your heroics. And it's never a good idea to render a back slap because a misplaced whack can cause a food chunk to head in the wrong direction, to slide farther down the throat, even into the lungs.

Herbal Cigarettes

Don't get fired up about toking herbal cigarettes. Okay, Okay, they're not addictive, but stick a lighted anything in your face and there'll be problems, like inflammation of the mouth lining, which could lead to disfiguring, even fatal, mouth and throat cancer. Cigarettes, no matter what they're made of, burn at a low temperature, which creates tars, other cancer-causing chemicals, and harmful gases, like carbon monoxide.

Herbal cigarettes and herbal snuff, because they don't contain nicotine or tobacco, aren't subject to laws barring their sales to minors, nor do they have to print health warnings on packaging.

Herbal Skin Creams

Some Chinese herbal skin creams, marketed as eczema cures, contain the steroid dexamethanone (illegal without a prescription in the United States) that has side effects ranging from worsened skin conditions to liver damage. A 1999 *British Medical Journal* article sounds an alarm about some health food stores in this country that carry herbal skin creams. But it's hard, if not impossible, to tell if they contain the outlawed steroid since few of the bottles list ingredients. Steer clear so your skin will be.

High-Definition Television

Cardiac monitors in a Dallas hospital fritzed out when a local television station began broadcasting high-definition television in the spring of 1998. The TV signals messed up the hospital's cardiac monitors' electrical systems by operating on the same radio spectrum. Nobody was hurt during the incident but experts, noting the interference caused by microwave oven and cell phone emissions, which have interrupted anti-lock brakes and other electronic auto systems, caution that problems may occur in the future.

Home Canning

Put up and throw up.

Grandma's peach preserves can be a killer jam. Botulism is a virulent toxin (1 teaspoon is enough to snuff out 100,000 people) that lurks in improperly prepared and stored home-canned food. To put food up safely is a megillah—levels of heat, acidity, and cleanliness have to be on target, jars must be sterile and airtight, temperatures just so.

Keep Granny away from the kitchen and down at the bowling alley where she belongs.

Home Fitness Equipment

Stationary bicycles, treadmills, and ski machines loll around in about a third of all American homes. The exercise machines do more than catch dust; they render bodily harm, especially to children's tiny fingers and hands.

The Consumer Product Safety Commission reports that in 1996, seventeen people were killed and more than 32,000 received emergency treatment for home fitness-equipment injuries, which included amputations, lacerations, abrasions, and fractures. About half the wounded were children younger than fifteen years.

You know what to do: Keep kids away from the equipment;

store the machinery in a safe place or make it inoperable when you're not around; buy spokeless stationary bikes, and while you're spinning your wheels, read the safety manual. Better still, join a gym.

Horseback Riding

About 70,000 equestrians trot into emergency rooms each year, and apparently, getting hurt is as easy as falling off a horse, which is how people wind up saddled with sprains, dislocations, and fractures of the neck, back, arms, and legs.

Leading a nag to water should never be treated as horseplay, especially by kids, many of whom are hurt during grooming and feeding times. The *Journal of Family Practice* says that almost two-thirds of all horsey injuries can be attributed to the animals' behavior and actions, which could help justify why Trigger was stuffed.

Hospitals

Staph happens.

Hospitals are germy places, full of bedpans, blood, and ooze, so it shouldn't come as a surprise that every year about 2 million people pick up a bug while they are hospitalized. What might give you pause is that, annually, more Americans die from hospital-acquired infections than from car wrecks and homicides combined.

What should offend you is the laziness of health care workers when it comes to washing their hands. Study after study shows that this first-line defense against spreading disease is notoriously ignored by hospital staffs. A recent investigation, conducted by Duke University, found that only 17 percent of physicians who treated patients in an intensive care unit appropriately washed up. Miffed about the lax hygiene practices, *The New England Journal of Medicine* rants: "Experts in infection control coax, cajole, threaten, and plead and still their colleagues neglect to wash their hands."

Scary is knowing that antibiotics can't always save the day; 70 percent of all hospital-borne infections are caused by antibiotic-resistant microbes that have responded to pharmaceutical assaults by mutating and hanging tough. Superbugs rule.

(See *Doctors' Writing; Stethoscopes*)

Hot Baths

About 70 people meet scalding deaths and hundreds more are badly burned every year while scrub-a-dubbing. If you can't stand the heat, get out of the kitch...er, tub.

Hot Dogs

The cure's a bitch. Nitrites, used to process some hot dogs, can combine with substances that are found in other foods and in the stomach to form potent cancer-causing chemicals, called nitrosamines. Doctors at the University of Southern California School of Medicine have linked a small number of cases of childhood leukemia to nitrite-laden hot dogs, but the wienies over at the Department of Agriculture haven't called for an alternative method of curing the meats.

Americans wolf down an average of sixty hot dogs a year—a stunning gastronomical statistic considering the products' ingredients: animal snouts, lips, intestines, and spleens. Consumer complaints made to the USDA about "foreign-object contamination" in hot dogs include items that don't cut the mustard, like stiff hog hairs, pieces of glass, screws, rubber bands, and black grease.

In 1999, hundreds of hot doggers were infected with listeria, the bacteria that takes no prisoners; millions of contaminated hot dog packages were subsequently recalled from store shelves. During another notorious outbreak, fifteen people died and six suffered miscarriages or stillbirths after eating listeria-tainted hot dogs. Best way to kill the germ is by thoroughly cooking hot dogs (five minutes of boiling, ten minutes grilling), which, unfortunately, won't rid the wieners of screws and rubber bands.

(See *Brie; Deli Meats*)

Hot Food

Chill the swill.

Piping hot food and drinks can burn delicate tissues on the way down the gullet. Beware especially of microwaved foods, nags *The New England Journal of Medicine* after doctors tended to several patients with thermal injuries to the esophagus—the tube from the throat to the stomach—they received after drinking soups and beverages heated in the fast-cook ovens. The center of microwaved food and drinks is actually much hotter than the outside, so cool them down before guzzling.

Hot Showers

Damp and rosy-skinned, you may feel freshly laundered, but actually you're flush with bacteria. Even the steamiest shower water doesn't kill germs, and dousing warm could cause bacterial growth on your bod. Cold showers serve more than one purpose. Splash nippy, and banish (at least temporarily) those hooligans with a loofah sponge.

(See *Loofahs*)

Hot Tubs

Hot tubs are big petri dishes, breeding all types of groddy bacteria. Pseudomonas, the least offensive of the wild bunch, cause ear infections and a perky rash doctors call "hot tub buns." A much more troublesome tub-spun bug, *Legionella bacteria,* grooves on hot water, flutters through the air and can become a deadly menace. In the early nineties, a cruise ship hot tub cultivated Legionnaire's disease which sickened some fifty passengers, sending one to Davy Jones's locker. A few years later, twenty-three visitors to a Virginia hot-tub showroom were infected with the muy malo disease; the victims, including two who died, were never even tub-immersed. They were infected just by being in the same hot-watered, bacteria-churning environment.

The National Institutes of Health is an even bigger wet blanket when it comes to hot tubs, spreading the news that the herpes virus can survive for several hours on the plastic-coated benches usually found near the steamy baths. Even the most chlorine-disinfected, germ-free tubs can be dangerous: the hot, swirling waters dilate blood vessels and raise body temperatures, which forces the heart to pump harder. Hot tubbers have experienced bouts of dehydration, nausea, and extreme weakness. Injuries from slips, falls, and near drownings send about 5,000 water-shriveled bodies slogging to hospital emergency rooms every year.

Hotel Rooms

Men leave them tidier but get locked out of hotel rooms naked more often than women, says an Australian survey. No matter your gender, or pajama and housekeeping habits, your home away from home could be raunchy. Using ultraviolet lighting, a forensic scientist uncovered blood, semen, and other bodily fluids on many of the purportedly "clean" sheets, blankets, and bedspreads in a number of Baltimore hotel rooms. Yecch. It's possible, says the Johns Hopkins School of Public Health, to get infected with hepatitis viruses from soiled bed linens, as well as to pick up a case of body lice, an easy-to-transmit varmint that burrows in mattresses and covers. Yecch redux.

Next hotel visit, strip off the bedspread—never lie on it—and make sure the sheets are clean and fresh. Don't pad around barefoot since hotel bathroom floors play host to athlete's foot fungi.

Enjoy your stay.

Hugging Daddy

Affectionate hugs could rub some kids the wrong way. As reported in the journal *Pediatrics*, an otherwise normal two-year-old boy developed pubic hair, acne, and an enlarged penis after exposure to the testosterone cream used by his body-building father to increase his muscle mass. The brawny unguent, sold only on the black market in the United States, contained the hormone responsible for the development of male sex organs and secondary sexual characteristics, like facial hair. The little boy had absorbed the cream through contact with his beefy dad, a daily user of the hormonal emollient. Within four months of ceasing the child's exposure to the testosterone cream, the prepubescent boy's macho symptoms had diminished, except for his penile size.

(See *Gray Beards*)

Humidifiers

Satire and martinis are best served dry. Indoor air is not.

Moisturizing humidifiers help rid a room of skin-cracking parched air, but at the same time, could cultivate a hearty crop of unhealthy fungi on your sofa. To prevent your décor from taking on a chia-pet mien, use mineral water in a humidifier, change it every day, and keep the humidity level lower than 60 percent.

Ice Cream

Not tonight, dear, I've got a double-dip chocolate mocha.

"Brain freeze" is the intense head-grabbing pain that kicks in when Arctic-cold ice cream hits the roof of the mouth, causing the brain's blood vessels to swell. The eye-numbing headache, suffered by at least a third of ice cream eaters, can last as long as five minutes. Although mostly harmless, ice cream headaches can sometimes touch off migraines. To melt away the chance of brain freeze, don't lick so quick.

Ice Cubes

E. coli, spread by fecal contamination, can knock you cold. Always wash up before filling or emptying ice trays. Here's another cool tip: Next hotel visit, spring for room-service ice instead of scooping it out of the ice bin down the hall. You don't know whose hands have been rummaging around the cubes.

Impotence

Whether you're up for it or not, doctors at Loyola University Medical Center say that impotence may be the first sign of heart disease.

Men with penile blood flow problems are more inclined to show cardiac abnormalities, even if they have no other symptoms, and should undergo a thorough health exam before taking medications to firm up their problem.

Internet

The first investigation of the Internet's effect on users' psychological well-being shook up researchers as well as corporate sponsors, which included some high-tech honchos. The surprise results: The Web's a virtual downer.

Internet users who spend even a few hours a week online are more depressed, isolated, and lonely than those who log on less frequently. Net cruising, e-mailing, and chatrooming replace human communication, and are no match for reality bytes, claim researchers at Carnegie Mellon University after studying home-computer-using families. The more Web-corresponding the study subjects did, the less they chatted with family members or kept up with friends, and the more depressed they became. Dr. Sara Kiesler, professor of social and decision sciences, says that on-liners may be substituting cyberfriendships for stronger, real-life relationships. "You don't have to deal with unpleasantness, because if you don't like somebody's behavior, you can just log off."

It's friends and relatives—sometimes troublesome, always problematic—who play important roles in a person's life (more so than disembodied cyberpals), who offer close-at-hand support, and provide a sense of psychological security.

You might long for a delete button when dealing face-to-face with a mother-in-law, but it's the stuff of real life that keeps us connected, tied to friends and relations.

(See *Friends and Relations; Personal Computers*)

Intersections

Put a stop to it.

Drivers who breeze through red-lighted intersections cause a quarter million accidents every year. It's a lethal gamble: fatal crashes involving red-light running have increased 15 percent in recent years, according to a 1998 study by the Insurance Institute for Highway Safety. Offenders tend to be younger, with poor driving records and histories of alcohol use—responsible types who belong behind the wheel of two-ton vehicles.

Smile, the lane ranger may be watching. Some states use cameras to nab violators, ticketing them via mail.

January

Facial tissues and hearts flutter during January. The month marks the height of flu season (when hanky sales are at their highest) and it's also the time of year when the number of heart attacks hits a peak. It's a killer month: In the span of the first thirty-one days of the year, more deaths are recorded than during the other months.

Happy New Year.

(See *Cold Weather; Winter*)

January Birthdays

Make a wish...that you'd been born in December. People who leave the womb in January are twice as likely to be depressed in adult life as those born in the last month of the year. The American Psychological Society reports that the symptoms may be caused by holiday stress in the mother, the harmful effects of reduced daylight, or seasonal illnesses, like influenza, all of which can affect an unborn child.

Jerky

The can-be-lethal *E. coli* bacteria has been found in venison jerky. An Oregon outbreak of food poisoning was traced to the hides of deer slaughtered by hunters. Call it Bambi's revenge.

(See *Deer*)

Jewelry

When men with comb-overs sport harpooned ears, it's a sure bet that body piercing has lost completely its cachet. Truth be told, the only ones clucking over the it's-so-over trend are dentists and dermatologists, who fret about the health hazards of lanced tongues and honeycombed nipples.

Skin docs worry about the significant rise in allergic reactions to nickel, the metal most used in inexpensive jewelry, which can cause itching, swelling, and, ewww, crusting. Dentists wag about the dangers of oral piercing, not the least of which are the risks of developing nasty infections, choking on loose jewelry parts, shattering teeth, developing blood clots, and contracting hepatitis from unsterilized needles.

Your uvula or vulva, or whatever, may be hole-free, but you're still at risk for a gem-dandy injury. In 1997, the estimated 54,720 people treated in emergency rooms for bauble boo-boos (besides the infected piercings-gone-bad) included lots of kiddos with bead-clogged orifices, and adults with swollen ring-stuck fingers.

Jimsonweed

Wild-growing jimsonweed can be an extremely toxic trip. The New Jersey Poison Control Center recently reports that five kids ate the plant's seeds and became critically ill with hallucinations and seizures. It's loco to fool around with this stuff.

Juice Bars

Joints that hawk nutrient-packed fruit and veggie drinks may also be selling you a lemon. Many juice bars offer expensive megadosed beverages that are spiked with anywhere from 1,000 to 3,000 percent of the recommended daily allowance of vitamins and minerals. Save your money; you'll just be pissing it away—literally. Water-soluble vitamins are quickly eliminated through the urine, but before they're tinkled away, the monster doses of vitamins could do some major damage. Large hits of vitamin C, for instance, can cause nausea and diarrhea, and, quite possibly, kidney stones.

(See *Apple Juice; Grapefruit Juice*)

July

July will never win any safety awards. Drownings and poisonings take more American lives in the midsummer month than during any other time of the year. Around every Fourth of July, an estimated 10,000 people are treated in emergency rooms (already swamped with scores of the mangled and soon-to-be-dead from alcohol-related car wrecks) for burns and other brutalities inflicted by fireworks.

The cult of barbecue also makes July an ominous month. Hot-weather cookouts and picnics lure party-crashing bacteria. The unwelcomed bugs usually arrive via sloppy food handling. Know any backyard chefs who use a meat thermometer to ensure the doneness of grilled chicken or a burger? Or picnickers who wash their hands before fondling an ear of corn? Didn't think so. Recent studies prove that most people really don't know much about food safety. In one survey, about 70 percent of interviewed picnickers admitted they stored food coolers in a hot, disease-breeding car trunk rather than tucking them inside the safety of an air-conditioned vehicle; 40 percent never soap-and-water cleaned their coolers between outings.

Brisket-and-booze fests are emergency room visits waiting to happen. Impatient, pie-eyed barbecuers sling lighter fluid on uncooperative charcoal and whoosh! singed hair, if they're lucky, but all too often the chefs are flame broiled with second- and third-degree burns. Appoint a designated cook.

(See *Summer; Well-Done Meat*)

Kentucky

Maybe it's all that bluegrass. According to a government mental health survey, Kentuckians, more than any other states' residents, don't feel completely with it for an average of five days a month.

If you're allergic to secondhand smoke, steer clear (or your lungs won't be) of the state that boasts the highest share of tokers. And don't expect KY to turn the world on with its smile: More than 40 percent of the state's inhabitants over the age of sixty-five are toothless.

(See *Squirrels*)

Keys

Swallowing keys is a kid thing; so is getting a charge out of poking the metal chunks into electrical sockets. Adults know better; they use keys and key chains to scratch their corneas, slash fingers, and lacerate scalps, or to set off Mace-spraying key chain attachments to temporarily blind their eyes.

Grown-ups had a lock on the vast majority of the almost 4,000 key-related, treatment-requiring accidents in 1997.

Kissing a Dog

Pooch smooching transmits all sorts of unfriendly parasites, bacteria, viruses, and fungi. Each year, more than a million Americans get roundworms, hookworms, pinworms, and tapeworms from bussing their canine pals.

In humans, since parasitic infections are almost impossible to diagnose (we tend not to scoot across the carpet on our behinds), people often never discover why they're sick with headaches, liver ailments, or sinus infections.

Can't worm your way out of this one. Teach Rover to shake.

(See *Dogs*)

Kneeling

Genuflection may be good for the soul but it's hell on patellas. Pray you won't suffer bursitis of the knee. The painful inflammation of the joint-protecting fluid sac is called (in pre-femlib lingo) "housemaid's knee." For kneeling comfort, the *Mayo Clinic Health Letter* recommends cushioning pads.

Lakes

Jump in a lake, come out with a bellyache. It's not slithering reptiles you have to worry about. Instead, swim clear of diapered toddlers. Potentially lethal bacteria, like *E. coli*, which is transmitted by human fecal matter, can contaminate popular swimming lakes, which unlike public pools, aren't regulated or treated for water quality and could be teeming with poopy germs.

Lakes can also harbor microorganisms, which thrive in warm, fresh water. *Naegleria fowleri* amoebae, if inhaled, can infect the human brain. Primary amebic meningoencephalitis, a disease that occurs more commonly during the summer months, is difficult to treat and can result in death within a week.

Diving accidents are the fourth leading cause of spinal injuries. Lakes, with hidden rocks, tree stumps, and debris, are headfirst catastrophes waiting to happen. Dive safely.

(See *Fishing; Water Parks*)

Landing a Punch

Listen up bullies. Punch someone upside the head and you could be the one in a world of hurt. Doctors who studied fisticuffers at New

York's St. Luke's–Roosevelt Hospital found that knuckle-rapped patients who waited at least two days before seeking treatment had to endure long hospital bouts, and some sluggers suffered permanent disabilities. How come? Bacteria in a human's mouth is extremely virulent, and without quick treatment, serious infection sets in, which could cause heavy scarring. Who needs to see the other guy?

Laundry

Putting an entirely different spin on laundry, microbiologist Dr. Charles Gerba of the University of Arizona discovered that disgusting rascals, such as fecal bacteria, salmonella, and hepatitis A, can infiltrate washing machines.

The laundry skullduggery happens since few Americans—some industry guesses stand at only 5 percent—use hot water or bleach to clean clothes, and, too, because wash and dry cycles have been shortened by manufacturers. The rigors of laundry have become so pantywaist that harmful bacteria and viruses are able to survive and remain on clothes. The greatest threat of fecal contamination comes when people transfer wet laundry to the dryer and spread the malevolent bacteria to their hands and, later, to food preparation.

The anal retentive Dr. Gerba offers a few of his own washday hints: launder undies last to prevent the spread of *E. coli*, and, fairly often, run an empty washing machine with just bleach to kill any lingering bacteria.

(See *Clothespins*)

Leaf Blowers

Gasoline-powered leaf blowers are polluting and noisy. Tilting the decibel level at 120, blasting as loud as an ambulance siren, the annoying lawn tenders have been banned in neighborhoods in some parts of the country. Crank a leaf blower long enough, your hearing will be gone with the wind.

(See *Yard Work*)

Leaky Pipes

A plague on your house. The medical journal, *Caduceus,* speculates that the last of the ten calamities to befall ancient Egypt was actually poisonous mold, the same vile crud skulking in modern-day houses.

Toxic mold, colonizing in water that collects around leaky pipes, may pester you with ailments like skin rashes, sleep disorders and migraine headaches. Vet your house: Fix the leak, use bleach to kill the mold, and prepare for the coming onslaught of locusts, boils, and frogs.

Leather Jackets

It's patently true that some people are highly sensitive to chemicals used to tan and color animal hides. If you're scratching and wheezing like crazy, go beyond the fringe and forgo leather jackets, sandals, bracelets, and the like.

Leftovers

Microwave adios to warmed-up leftovers. The plastic that's wrapped around food could be a tumor monger, according to one school of scientific thought. An ingredient often used in some household clingy wraps—and most grocery store–wrapped meat and cheese—is the plasticizer DEHA, which can migrate into food (especially high-fat-content meat and cheese) and, say some food safety experts, can ruffle the body's hormonal balance.

Take off the clingy wrap from store-bought meat and cheese before storing them in the refrigerator. Better idea: Have the butcher wrap that T-bone in paper, and buy your mozzarella from a cheese wheel.

Watch what you heat: Never let clingy wrap touch your victuals while in the microwave.

Leis

Aloh-ouch. Hawaii's gracious custom of presenting visitors with blossomy laurels could lay you up, advises the *British Medical Journal*. The neck of a lei-wearing tourist became painfully blistered on the flight home from the island paradise when her flower necklace touched off an allergic reaction.

Licorice

Licorice has been used for centuries as a cold remedy, tummy settler, and asthma treatment. But in some people, the fennel-tasting food can upset the body's chemical balance. High blood pressure, lung congestion, potassium depletion, and an irregular heartbeat are possible reactions to glycrrhizin, the oddly spelled chemical found in licorice. The frightening physical symptoms typically occur when a susceptible person eats an ounce a day on a regular basis. Since safe or beneficial dosages of licorice have yet to be determined, some medical experts, like The *University of California at Berkley Wellness Letter,* advise it's best not to eat it at all.

To men, the candy won't seem dandy at all if a recent claim by Italian physicians holds true. *The New England Journal of Medicine* reports that eating licorice root may decrease men's testosterone levels, which could impede sexual performance and cause a loss of sex drive.

(See *Chewing Gum*)

Lifeguarding

Give up your day job if it's lifeguarding an indoor pool. The notion that it's a safe profession has been blown right out of the water.

In recent tests, itchy eyes, sore throats, and irritated skin were common complaints of lifeguards at sixty-three swimming pools that measured high levels of nitrogen trichloride, a gas formed when disinfecting chlorine mixes with human perspiration and urine. The gas, trapped indoors, not allowed to escape, becomes more concentrated, and could cause long-term health consequences.

In another study, lifeguards blew the whistle on water sprays that spew illness-causing bacteria through the air—the very air they breathe at work all day. The germ-tossing sprays, reports *The Lancet*, have caused pool-related coughs, chest tightness, and fever. The medical journal cautions that given the popularity of water sprays at indoor pools, other outbreaks of "lifeguard lung" are likely.

(See *Water Parks*)

Lightning

Nature can be a mother. Lightning bolts smack the earth 100 times each second, sparking with 50,000° F, reaching almost 5 miles in length. It's a helluva wallop that crispy critters up to 400 people every year. Now scientists have come up with a striking new theory: lightning as stealth killer.

Usually, lightning clobbers someone with a direct hit, or it slams into the ground, then shimmies over to where the person's standing, and *Pow!* Toast. The force of nature can be with you: It's believed that lightning can stop a heart cold without ever leaving telltale marks or burns if the skybolt's electrical current zaps a body precisely during a sensitive heartbeat stage in the cardiac cycle.

(See *Thunderstorms; Underwire Bras*)

Liposuction

No ifs, ands, or butts, flab removal is one popular and growing business. Liposuction rids women of the evil that is cellulite—the dreaded dimple of doom. In record numbers, men are falling over their double chins to have the fat-sucking surgery. The American Society of Plastic and Reconstructive Surgeons reports liposuction

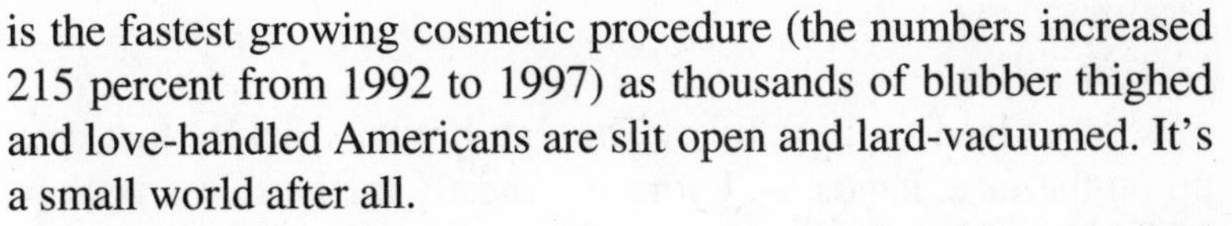

is the fastest growing cosmetic procedure (the numbers increased 215 percent from 1992 to 1997) as thousands of blubber thighed and love-handled Americans are slit open and lard-vacuumed. It's a small world after all.

Choose your fat sucker with care. Anybody with a medical degree can hang a lipo shingle, and after little more than a weekend course, can begin performing the delicate procedure. Cosmetic surgery, a specialty that's virtually unregulated, is getting crowded with doctors who may have no surgical training. What's the attraction? Lipo has proved to be extremely lucrative for physicians; since most insurance plans won't cover the procedure, it's a cash up-front deal, a greenback magnet for all types of doctors—obstetricians, family practitioners, dermatologists, oral surgeons—who, with dwindling incomes from their own specialties and financially hobbled by managed care companies, are in fierce competition for butterball patients.

Unfortunately, there's no such thing as national or statewide data on complications and deaths from liposuction—they aren't compiled. Know that the risks of the procedure are sizable. Blundered operations can leave ugly scars and injure internal organs; during the 1990s, an estimated 100 people croaked from complications, such as massive infections, perforated organs, or fluid in the lungs, usually because the doctor wasn't trained, took out too much fat, pumped in too much anesthetic-laced saline solution, or used dirty surgical implements.

Before you slip under the knife, or vacuum as the case may be, do some legwork. Find an experienced physician, preferably a board-certified *plastic* surgeon with impeccable credentials, or take the novel approach: accept your not-so-perfect body the way it is.

Lipstick

Cruising for a makeover? Kiss off that idea. The Denver police report the demise of a behind-the-wheel-primper, who braked suddenly, swallowed her tube of lipstick, and choked to death.

Gussy up at home.

Liver Spots

Few of us lead spotless lives. The flat, brown speckles that crop up on the face, hands, and arms are mostly the harmless wallops of middle-age. But liver spots, caused by years of sun exposure, can be precursors of melanoma, the sometimes-deadly skin cancer. So, old-timer, have a dermatologist check out those age spots.

Lizards

No 3 A.M. barking fits or smelly litter boxes—lizards seem perfect low-maintenance house pets, but the varmints are crawling with salmonella. Remember those tiny pet-shop turtles, the ones you kept in a water bowl festooned with plastic palm trees? They're not for sale anymore, yanked off the market because they, like lizards, carry the same innards-cramping, vomit-producing bacteria.

Lizards nearly always test positive for salmonella, and if allowed to roam, the reptiles will track the ill-mannered bacteria all over the house. The National Center for Infectious Diseases pleads with lizard owners to wash their hands after handling the cold-blooded pets; if not, the agency says it's like "finger painting the house with salmonella." Lizart!

(See *Cats; Dogs; Hedgehogs; Parakeets*)

Long Faces

You might fit the profile. A narrow face with a jawbone that extends too low makes breathing through the nose difficult, says the Academy of General Dentistry, theorizing that the shape of your mug relates to certain health problems. People with short kissers and small jawbones are more vulnerable to temporomandibular joint syndrome (the infamous TMJ) that causes jaw pain, headaches, and earaches.

(See *Chubby Cheeks; Fat Necks*)

Long Hours

Economists declare that most Americans are putting in longer hours at work. The average person now labors 44 hours a week; since 1977, the amount of time spent on the job per week has increased by 3.5 hours.

The work week for an average couple is 1.5 days longer now than it was in the 1960s. More women are working, employed at full-time rather than part-time jobs, and men are punching more clock hours, too.

So, work never killed anyone. Right? Wrong, argue Japanese medical researchers, whose case studies recognized a definite association between the number of monthly working hours and the risk of acute myocardial infarction: The longer the hours worked, the greater the risk for heart attack.

Employers may not have to worry about the day-care issue if their female employees work considerable overtime. Thai and Danish researchers report that putting in more than 70 hours a week may make it more difficult for women to conceive a child.

Long Underwear

The fabric of your life is a comfy fit, except during the icy rigors of winter sports. Cotton knickers do nothing but soak up perspiration to keep your skin damp and clammy. You're not only miserable, your body wastes energy trying to stay warm, so there's a good risk of hypothermia. Baby, when it's cold outside, slip into synthetic dainties.

Loofahs

A good scrub with a loofah sponge softens your skin, but could rub you the wrong way. The *Journal of Clinical Microbiology* advises that loofahs are a favorite hangout for bacteria that can trigger skin eruptions. Don't be a doofus; dry your loofah out after each use, and decontaminate it with bleach once a week.

(See *Hot Showers*)

Love Connections

Doing the wild thing can give rise to seminal problems.

Some lovers tend to bear down when coupling, which makes them lose their memory. Doctors at Johns Hopkins Medical Institution say that sometimes nookie straining creates intense pressure in the brain's blood vessels, which temporarily blocks blood flow to the central part of the brain; if this happens, the paramour can have up to 12 hours of amnesia and may lose the ability to form new memories. The three-word endearment, "I love you," could very well become the confused, "Who are you?"

Love Handles

Practice waist management.

An average six-footer will add almost an inch, or 3.3 pounds of flab to his waist per decade. Besides needing a good tailor, the jelly bellied have an increased risk of health problems. Men with waists expanding more than 40 inches are nearly three times as likely to register high cholesterol, seven times more apt to be diabetic, and almost four times as likely to be in poor physical health as are wispier guys with waists smaller than 37 inches.

Full-figured gals don't fare any better. Women whose waists are 30 inches or wider run more than twice the risk of heart disease than the less rotund who measure 27 inches or smaller around the middle.

Low Cholesterol

Congratulations! You've lowered your off-the-chart cholesterol. Never mind. A new study shows that while high cholesterol raises the risk of strokes from blood clots in the brain, extremely low cholesterol can trigger strokes resulting from burst blood vessels in the brain.

Don't be so smug about your exceptionally low natural cholesterol level. You probably suffer from anxiety and depression. Yet another investigation, this one probing women between the ages of eighteen and twenty-seven, determined that of those with low cholesterol readings, 39 percent scored high to very high on a depression scale, and another 35 percent expressed high anxiety. Women with elevated levels of cholesterol had significantly lower tendencies for depression and anxiety.

Don't indulge your crème fraîche cravings just yet. Doctors still maintain that the health benefits of having low cholesterol far outweigh the potential risks.

Luggage

You think <u>you're</u> hauling a lot of baggage...what about the bruised and battered wayfarers who take trips to emergency rooms, hobbling with strained backs, necks, and knees from lifting heavy valises, with snapped bones after tripping over suitcases, crying over sliced fingers from sharp metal locks and pulled groins from toting carry-ons—all that misery without racking up any frequent flyer miles.

(See *Frequent Flying; Luggage Carts*)

Luggage Carts

Slingshotting off a bridge is a lot safer than unstrapping your luggage cart. Bungee cords are mean snappers. The elastic bands with metal hooks at each end have snapped back and ripped open eyes, causing dislocated lenses, internal bleeding, retinal detachment, and temporary loss of sight. Because they tear the tissue around the eye's drainage canal, bungee cord injuries can lead to future vision problems like glaucoma, a disease that can cause blindness. Writing in the *American Journal of Ophthalmology*, Dr. Louis Chorich, clinical assistant professor in ophthalmology at Ohio State University said, "Bungee cords are great tools... but I really don't think people realize how dangerous they can be."

(see *Frequent Flying; Luggage Carts*)

M

Maine's Route 201

It's called Moose Alley. Route 201 in northwestern Maine, a high-speed straightaway to Canada, with little to slow you down, except dazzling scenery and a likely run-in with a wayward moose.

Moose spell big bucks in Maine, where tourist safaris trample woodlands for a glimpse of one of the 30,000 magnificent beasts that roam the state. But accidents involving vehicles and the bulbous-nosed animals, some sporting six-foot antler racks, are now epidemic in Maine, which averages more than 600 moose-car accidents a year. Route 201 isn't the only stretch of road where driver and moose are likely to collide. Wildlife biologist Karen Morris admits it's a statewide problem, especially May through July when more moose and cars are on the move.

A car is no match for the 1,500 pound creature; encounters are usually catastrophic to both animal and human—about 15 percent of the motorists involved in a moose mishap require medical treatment, and the moose, faring no better, seldom survives. Unintimidated by vehicles, the dark-colored animals (often drawn to roads to lick the salt deposits left by snow-clearance crews) are hard to see and so tall that their eyes don't reflect in headlights. Unlike a car-struck deer, which is usually glanced off the side of a vehicle, the taller, heavier moose is hit at knee level, flipped up and through the windshield, usually with tragic results.

Alarmed by the human road kill, some Mainers want to cull the ungainly animals through looser hunting restrictions. Moose Maniacs soundly disagree, citing the tourist-revenue generating power of the iconic critter.

It's only a matter of time when other parts of the country will be facing the same moose-aplenty predicament. Because of curbs on hunting the creature, the elimination of natural predators (like the big, bad wolf), and the conversion of farmlands back to forests, more than a million moose are on the loose, loping through the northern United States, migrating southward.

Making Music

The chief objection to playing wind instruments is that it prolongs the life of the player.—George Bernard Shaw.

Almost not so for the teen trumpet player whose intense jam session played havoc with a congenital defect in his heart. The rooty-toot-tooter became temporarily paralyzed on one side of his body when the increased pressure from blowing into the instrument forced air bubbles to pass into his bloodstream to his brain, which caused a mini stroke.

Music-related injuries may seem out of tune, but one survey of 250 musicians notes that about half have had some musculoskeletal symptoms, like carpal tunnel syndrome, tendonitis, or bursitis, with complaints of pain, stiffness, tingling, numbness, and chronic muscle strain. Citing overuse injuries as the most common, the Johns Hopkins Medical Institution harps on the notion that almost every player will suffer shoulder pain severe enough to seek medical attention during a musical career.

(See *Playing Rock and Roll*)

Male Pattern Baldness

A chrome dome could spell doom. Male pattern baldness, the spreading barren spot on the crown of the head, is the most common form of hair loss. It's also a risk factor for heart disease. In a baldness-pattern research probe, the risk of heart disease increased as the head hair decreased. Of the 19,000 men in the study, all under the age of forty-five, the fellows with the most severe cases of bald pates had a 36 percent increased risk of heart disease. Frontal hair losers and receding hairliners had only about a 9 percent increased susceptibility for cardiac troubles.

The American Heart Association says that the bleak findings should concern men with severe baldness patterns who also have other heart disease risk factors, such as high cholesterol and high blood pressure.

Malls

Shopping for a drop-dead look? Go to the mall.

Heart attacks that strike in public places happen most often in high-stress areas, such as retail malls, casinos, and airports. First order of business is to survive the shopping bustle, then deal with the hustle. Reports of armed robberies, sexual attacks, and muggings are creating shopping mauls. Today's average shopping center has more crime than its 1978 counterpart—about seven times as many shoplifts and triple the number of parking lot crimes, alleges a Florida study. Spending just 74 cents per square foot on security (compared to $4.54 on routine maintenance), retail complexes, designed with nooks and crannies, secluded hallways, light-blocking trees, and dark parking decks seem to serve as a criminal's playground.

Caveat emptor indeed.

(See *Shopping Carts*)

Mangoes

It takes two to mango. Sap from the tropical fruit contains resins similar to those found in poison ivy and poison oak. If you're sen-

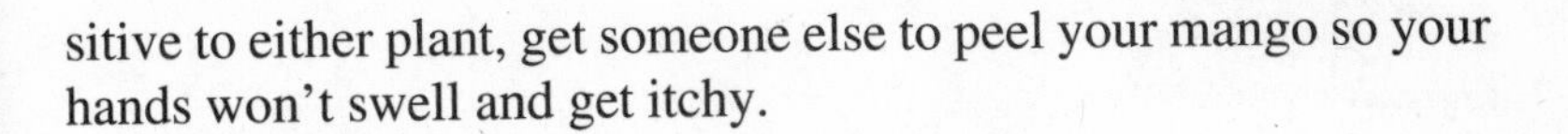
sitive to either plant, get someone else to peel your mango so your hands won't swell and get itchy.

Maraschino Cherries

Maraschino cherries, preternaturally crimson and sickly sweet, are the fruits of chemistry.

Harvested cherries are soaked in a microbe-killing solution of sulfur dioxide and lime up to six weeks, pitted, and bleached with sodium chlorite, then stored in a sodium bisulfite brine. The maraschinos-to-be, long robbed of any natural color and taste, are bathed with a sugar solution and scarlet dye before an almond-oil flavoring is added. Stem the urge to plop one atop an ice cream sundae.

(See *Red Food*)

Marital Spats

I do. No, you don't.

Domestic tiffs bruise more than feelings. Marital spats send blood pressures soaring and heartbeats racing, especially when partners consider themselves equals.

A University of Utah canvass of forty-five married couples discovered that during an argument, the men and women who battled evenly on the same power grid had significantly higher spikes in their blood pressure readings than did those who considered themselves the dominant partner. The submissive spouses who gave into their partner's opinions had only a slight escalation in their vital signs.

The study concluded that during a squabble it takes less effort to resolve conflict when one partner rules the roost and the other gives in, than when both spouses regard themselves as dominant, never-say-die players.

Marshmallows

Care for a little barbecue sauce on those marshmallows? Why not? The squishy treats are made with gelatin refined from cattle hide and bones. Vegans or those allergic to beef should round up less-bovine confections.

Martinis

The venerable martini: Shaken, not stirred; sipped, not gulped.

The oaf who ignored that bit of spiritual counsel chug-a-lugged his martini, including the onion-garnished toothpick, which punctured the back of his throat. When the guzzler tried to cough up the wooden sliver, it got stuck up his nose. *The New England Journal of Medicine* reports a forceps-wielding doctor successfully removed the offending toothpick.

Wouldn't 007 be proud?

Mascara

Share your toys and your wealth, but bogart your mascara. If not, it's a germ swap.

Be extravagant as well as selfish. After three months of solo use, when the mascara wand's bacteria-fighting preservatives have pooped out, toss it out and buy a fresh one.

Mattresses

Lie down with dogs...

Stockholm researchers vacuumed fresh-from-the-factory mattresses and showroom demo beds (some still plastic-wrapped) and ferreted out traces of dog, cat, and other animal allergens. The tidy Swedes assumed that the allergens were tracked in by pet-owning factory workers.

Medical Consent Forms

The femur ossicle is consociated and juxtapositional to the innominate skeletal structure in the lumbar region. Translation: The thigh bone's connected to the hip bone.

Medical consent forms, granting permission to doctors to do god-knows-what to your body, are pure gibberish. The clear-as-mud documents are so complicated, garbled with hard-to-understand words, rambling sentences, and perplexing jargon that it helps to earn a Ph.D. before plowing through the gobbledygook, so says the medical journal *Surgery*. Reviewing more than 600 consent forms from hospitals around the country, researchers found that to understand most forms, patients, at the very least, need a high school education; to comprehend about a fourth of the documents requires a college education. Even more frustrating is the finding that most of the medical consent forms don't include the kind of patient information that you'd likely want to know, like alternatives to surgery.

Medicine Cabinets

Medicine cabinets are degrading places, not fit for potions and pills. Storing drugs in the heat and humidity of bathrooms or kitchens can diminish the potency and effectiveness of prescription and over-the-counter medications. There's even a good chance the muggy conditions could render them toxic. Keep your stash in a cool, dry dresser drawer, far away from children's reach.

(See *Toothbrushes*)

The Midwest

According to data collected by the U.S. Department of Health and Human Services, the number of visits to emergency rooms is higher in the Midwest than in the South or the West.

Midwesterners are more likely to smoke and be overweight

and also admit in larger numbers to drinking while they're driving, which, hello! might account for all the hospital visits.

Mineral Oil

Don't take it lying down. A nighttime dose of mineral oil shouldn't be swallowed before bedtime. If the oil is somehow regurgitated and then inhaled into the lungs, it can crank up a bad disease called lipoid pneumonia.

Miniblinds

A kid'll eat lead too. Some imported vinyl miniblinds contain lead, and after exposure to the sun, will deteriorate to form lead-laced dust. Children playing with the blinds have been poisoned when they put lead-covered fingers in their mouths. The Consumer Product Safety Commission recommends that parents of young children remove the miniblinds from their houses and shop for lead-free blinds.

Buy American.

Mobile Homes

A twister touches down and a trailer park goes up. Although news reports make it seem so, mobile homes really aren't tornado bait. It's that mobile dwellings rarely live up to their name; they aren't very, well, mobile. Venturing only from the showroom to the buyer's permanent site, the wheel estate comes to roost most often somewhere in the tornado-prone Sun Belt, which goes to explain why, over the last few years, close to half of all twister fatalities have been mobile homers.

The carnage-by-whirlwind occurs also because most manufactured homes—the industry-preferred term for the uninspiringly designed lodgings—rely on a system of metal straps to hug them close to terra firma during high winds. All too often, the anchoring system is missing or defective, and it's bye, bye Toto.

Although fires don't occur more often in manufactured homes, because the buildings' design and construction make flames spread faster, the mobile-homed are twice as likely to die from conflagrations as are occupants of other residences.

Molasses

Sweetly languid, molasses may contain preserving sulfites, which in some people cause breathing problems or hives, chest tightness, or even fatal anaphylactic shock. Pore over the label.

Mondays

As if you need another reason to dread them.

So sorrowful are the lyrics to Billie Holliday's bluesy lament, "Gloomy Sunday," they've actually driven the lovelorn to suicide. But Monday, not Sunday, is the day when most people take their own lives, says the American Association of Suicidology. It's lousy all the way around because Monday is also the day of the week when more heart attacks occur.

(See *Fridays; Saturdays; Weekends*)

Money

Money laundering isn't such a bad idea.

Coins and greenbacks are cruddy with bacterial colonies; the smaller the bill denomination, the grimier it is. To get to the root of the evil, a microbiology lab hit paydirt when it swabbed and cultured moolah, uncovering disease-carrying varmints like scuzzy fecal bacteria, food-poisoning staphylococcus, skin-infecting *Staphylococcus aureus,* and acne-making propionibacteria. "Money is truly dirty," concludes *The Journal of the American Medical*

Association. If your immune system is humming along, chances are you won't get sick from the filthy lucre, but heed Mom's admonition about hands in mouths.

Tests of $20 bills have given currency to money's other dirty little secret. Cash is doped up, too, snowed under with cocaine. Contamination rates of examined bills have been as high as 100 percent and the *Journal of Forensic Sciences* says: "...most Americans handle small amounts of cocaine every day, not as packets sold by drug dealers but on the dollar bills that line their pockets."

Monster Truck Shows

Monster truck shows attract millions of mayhem-loving spectators to watch drivers of five-ton, supercharged trucks—11 feet high, perched on tires that are taller than most men, with testeroned names like Black Widow, Terminator, and Towasaurus Rex—rev up 2,000-horsepowered, ozone-sucking engines and zoom around dirt-filled, gasoline-splashed arenas. The four-wheeled Rambos put on quite a show as they speed race, tug heavy loads, ram other muscle trucks before squashing them like empty beer cans, and as a grand finale Evel Knievel–leap over rows of salvage-yard cars. Imagine that.

Winter is prime time for the heavy-metal entertainment, but the hunky rigs belch so much carbon monoxide that indoor arena audiences have been forced to evacuate when the colorless, odorless gas was measured at dangerous levels. Quebec health officials banned monster truck shows entirely during winter months after excessive levels of carbon monoxide were recorded at several rallies. In low concentrations, CO first causes flulike symptoms—headaches, dizziness, and nausea; later, confusion and disorientation set in (already prerequisites for monster truck show attendance). Higher doses of the gas render victims unconscious and can lead to brain damage and death, which could be a sweet release after observing one of the free-wheeling shows.

Morning Coffee

Quaffing four or five cups of coffee in the A.M. greatly increases stress hormone levels, say Duke University researchers, who report that morning java junkies feel anxious well into the evening, a risky deal since stress hormones have been shown to increase the chance of heart damage.

Mornings

Getting out of bed in the morning is an act of false confidence. — Jules Feiffer.

Morning becomes no one. It's prime time for heart attacks and for strokes, which occur most often between 6 A.M. and noon.

Traffic-clogged early commutes jangle the nerves, and start the day with a wheeze and a hack from breathing smoke and pollution, in combo with pollen and mold (at their highest counts between 5 A.M. and 10 A.M.).

(See *Afternoons; Daytime; Nighttime*)

Mouthwash

Some mouthwash, spiked with a high-alcohol content, can dry out mucous membranes or rile a case of dry mouth. The National Cancer Institute says regular use of mouthwash that's more than 25 percent alcohol could increase the risk of mouth cancer.

Children, lured by the bright primary colors of mouthwash and undeterred by easy-open caps, have been poisoned from swallowing the pretty liquids.

Oral of the story? Hide mouthwash from young garglers.

Movie Previews

NIX MAX TRAX FLIX

Hollywood has broken all sorts of barriers: racial, sexual, and now thanks to distortion-free digital techno magic, sound. Movies are recorded louder, and coming attractions, a reel pain, are the loudest. How noisy are the flicks? First off, know that sound is measured in decibels; continued exposure to noise above 85 decibels will insidiously and permanently destroy hearing. Normal conversation measures between 40 and 60 decibels and a power saw whirrs at 95 decibels. An explosion-rocked scene on today's silver screen is an easy 120 to 130 decibels, compared to the bullet-riddled finale of the sixties shoot-em-up, *Bonnie and Clyde*, which wimped out at a mere 80 decibels.

Otolaryngologists at Washington University School of Medicine say that a long series of movie machine-gun rat-a-tat-tat can wreak long-term hearing damage. A significant number of Americans—about 28 million—are experiencing hearing problems; 35 percent of the cases are wholly or partially attributable to noise exposure, says the American Speech-Language-Hearing Association. A major cause of hearing loss is recreational noise—protracted exposure to yard tools, concerts, car stereos, and movie soundtracks.

Earplugs will help, especially during those full-throttle previews, but don't waste time bellyaching to the theater manager; ratcheting down the volume, while it tames the car chase screeches, only muffles the dialogue.

(See *Car Stereos; Earplugs; Rock Concerts; Soundtracks; Yard Work*)

Movie Theater Seats

You always identified with dwarf Sneezy. That's because movie theater seats are covered with cat allergens, sniffs the *New Zealand Medical Journal,* citing an investigation that collected kitty hair and dander from movie theater seats in high enough concentrations to incite asthma or allergic reactions.

Mowing the Lawn

Blade runners rejoice! If ever you wanted excuses not to mow the lawn, you got 'em. For starters, research shows that the activity is hard on the heart; in one study, lawn mowing, especially huffing behind a manual mower, raised the blood pressures and heart rates of people with coronary artery disease.

Not a heart patient? Okay, you can still weasel out of the chore—toss out a few facts. Each year 230,000 to 400,000 people are raked over in hospital emergency rooms from lawn mower injuries (the majority of the mangled are children younger than fifteen), from minor cuts to gaping wounds, serious eye injuries to burns and electrocution. Riding lawn mowers account for about 25,000 of the injuries and some 75 deaths. With blades whirling at 200 mph, a small riding mower generates three times the power generated by a .357 Magnum pistol and slings debris—nails, jagged pieces of metal, rocks—faster than a speeding bullet.

Need more ammo to holster your participation in lawn care? Read the entries for Brush Cutters, Cut Grass, Mulch, Roses, and Yard Work.

Mulch

How much wood chip can the wood chipper chip before . . . not mulch, says the *Journal of Occupational and Environmental Medicine*. Wood chip mulch is a prime breeding ground for plant, bacterial, and fungal gunk that can cause a flulike syndrome called "inhalation fever," with symptoms, like inflamed lung passages, chest tightness, muscle aches, and fever, which may not show up until four to six hours after shoveling the mulch.

Don't mask the problem. Wear one.

Munchies

Fridge-raiding snackers who pack away half or more of their daily calories after 7 P.M. could develop what psychologists call night-eating syndrome, which is marked by morning anorexia (not eating the next day) and insomnia.

Museums

A Baltimore museum encouraged young visitors to play with its hat collection. The interactive exercise gave some of the kids prickly doses of blood-sucking head lice.

Docent it make you sick?

Mushrooms

Every year, nearly 10,000 cases of mushroom poisoning turn up, with 90 percent caused by *Amanita,* a species commonly called the "death cap." It's difficult to distinguish from several edible varieties, so unless you want to find yourself in deep shiitakes, forage the greengrocer instead of the woods.

Mustaches

The upper lip as babe magnet? It's snot.

Mustaches trap allergy-aggravating pollen, claims the Mid-Atlantic Kaiser Permanente Medical Group, which persuaded a group of whiskered, allergic men to shampoo their lip hairs twice a day. After a few weeks, the hirsute fellows reported fewer sneezes, wheezes, and runny noses, so much so that they were able to cut back on their allergy medications.

(See *Close Shaves; Gray Beards*)

N

Nail Biting

Quick! Stop living hand to mouth. Gnawed fingernails look awful and all that nibbling might do as much physical damage as cosmetic ruin. Habitual chewers suffer frequent bacterial infections, warts, and painful inflammations that can deform fingers.

Nail Guns

It's a high-velocity *gun* loaded with *nails*. Get it? Toters of the pneumatic six-shooter apparently don't recognize the tool's ruthless action. Medical and construction trade journals circulate penetrating tales of the badly wounded trigger hapless, who suffer from self-inflicted shots to the groin, thighs, and brain.

Make your day: pay attention to warning labels, and ready, *aim*, fire with both hands.

Napping

You snooze, you lose.

A daily siesta could hasten the Big Sleep, reports the *Archives of Internal Medicine*. After studying the napping habits of 455 seventy-year-olds for 6.5 years, researchers concluded that the mortality rate of the lazybones who regularly took afternoon naps was nearly double that of the stay-awake participants.

(See Sleep)

Narcissists

Mirror mirror on the wall, who's the most dangerous of them all?

The milquetoast Mittys who may go bonkers and trade in a pocket protector for an Uzi? Nah, don't sweat the nerds; instead, keep a wary eye on the arrogant, superiority-oozing egotists, the ones who think they're all that. Criticize a narcissist and you could become a punching bag.

Studies at Case Western Reserve University and Iowa State University debunk the popular notion that low self-esteem causes aggression, and claim that narcissistic behavior—excessive self-love—can actually lead to increased violence.

Defining narcissists as "people who have a strong desire to regard themselves as superior beings," researchers assessed 540 college students and rated them on a narcissism scale. Each was then asked to write a brief essay, which was evaluated by a fictitious grader as either, "Great essay!" or the thumbs-down, "This is one of the worst essays I have read!" All the students were given the opportunity to punish the grader (not a real person but the students didn't know that) by delivering a painfully loud blast of noise with a push of a button. Students who rated high on the narcissism scale and received a lousy critique zapped the grader more often and more severely than the lower self-esteemed who didn't exhibit aggression toward the grader, no matter what the evaluation.

Narcissists, the study claims, want to defeat others they perceive as threats to their bloated egos.

Nevada

Viva! Las Vegas has the highest suicide rate in the nation, with Reno a close second. Visitors to Vegas also kill themselves at a higher rate; one in twenty-five—four times the national average—cash in their own chips.

New Clothes

Never-worn duds can release a stinky chemical that's used in some textile manufacturing. Tiny amounts of formaldehyde can cause eye irritation, respiratory problems, and with long-term exposure, possibly cancer.

Wash *then* wear.

New Jersey

But, officer, that *was* a hand signal. The Garden State's licensed drivers are a pissy lot. More than half are angry, reports the Automobile Association of America. Jersey road ragers, flipping obscene gestures, cursing, blocking lanes, and tailgating, cause at least 80,000 accidents every year.

New York City

You'll ♥ New York, especially in May. Lilacs, birdsong, the springtime carcass float.

May marks the peak of New York's "floater season," when more bodies (chilled and hidden beneath the murky surface all winter) pop to the surface of the city's rivers than at any other time of year; almost a quarter of the corpses plucked from waterways in 1997 were retrieved during the merry month. Canoers and kayakers should take care to avoid being capsized by some poor stiff, or upended by a floater who's been dislodged from underwater debris by Spring's fast-rushing river currents.

Good news. The New York police department's Harbor Unit reports that the annual body retrieval count, formerly in the hundreds, is now down to fewer than fifty, and credits the lower violent crime rate, safer waterfront equipment that protects dockworkers from an accidental tumble into the brink, and a strong economy for the river cleanup since many of the bodies are thought to be suicides.

Bad news. The city that never sleeps doesn't take much to handwashing either. Recent survey findings of public restroom users' hygiene habits tsk-tsks New Yorkers for having the nation's dirtiest hands.

Worse news. Visitors to NYC are 34 percent more likely to croak of a heart attack than if they'd bought a ticket to somewhere else. Well, living in the Apple's got to be healthier for the ticker, right? Fugedaboutit. Gotham residents' death rates from heart attack are 55 percent higher than the U.S. average.

Leave town. When New Yorkers visit outside the city, their risk of dying of a coronary drops 20 percent. What gives? Basing his conclusions on 20 million death certificates from 1985 to 1994, study author psychologist Dr. Nicholas Christenfeld blames the high death rates on the city's anxiety-provoking, stress-producing intensity.

Nightclub Floors

"Nightclub finger" sounds like a honky-tonk flip off but it's a medical condition aptly named by emergency room physicians at the Royal Liverpool University Hospital. It happens when patrons of dimly lit bistros, bothered by sticky gunk on the bottom of their shoes, discover too bloody late that the debris they're swiping off is actually broken glass.

The Liverpudlian doctors offer a solution to the dicey problem: declare dark nightclubs to be glass-free zones. Yeah, that'll happen.

Night Lights

Children who slumber with a night light may be more likely to grow up to be nearsighted than sleep-in-the-dark kids. University of Philadelphia researchers make the provocative claim that during the first two years of life, a night light's dim glow can interfere with the eyes' normal growth and skew their focusing ability.

Some eye specialists dismiss the bedtime story, finding it all

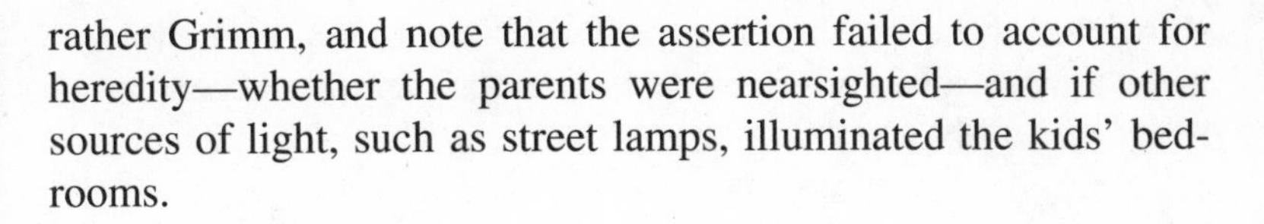

rather Grimm, and note that the assertion failed to account for heredity—whether the parents were nearsighted—and if other sources of light, such as street lamps, illuminated the kids' bedrooms.

Nightmares

A study dreamed up by Finnish researchers finds that people who have frequent nightmares are 15 percent more likely to be hospitalized at least once in their lifetime for mental illness.

Night Shifts

Day for night is a bad trade for the 20 million Americans who work at twenty-four-hour mail-order houses, computer service companies, hospitals, and factory assembly plants—the late-shift workers, who, on average, sleep two hours fewer a day than do nine-to-fivers. The little rack time the shifters get during the day is anything but restful—the phone rings, kids bicker, city noises intrude—and their bodies soon run up a hefty sleep debt, which we all wind up paying. Drowsy drivers are blamed for 100,000 crashes, 1,500 deaths, and 71,000 injuries every year. (In California, nearly half of all fatal highway accidents involve sleep-famished drivers.)

Sleep deprivation is estimated to cost $150 billion a year owing to workplace accidents and reduced productivity, reports the National Commission on Sleep Disorders Research. Two-thirds of all transportation accidents involving hazardous materials occur between 6 P.M. and 9 A.M., and industrial mishaps are twice as likely to occur on the night shift: Three of history's most notorious accidents—Three Mile Island, Bhopal, and Chernobyl—occurred during the "zombie zone," the hours between midnight and 4 A.M. when human energy and alertness levels dip the lowest.

Up to 75 percent of night-shifters complain about intestinal maladies, with symptoms from appetite loss to flatulence. Studies show that those on the graveyard shift are more susceptible to heart attacks, obesity, and depression, and are 60 percent more likely to get divorced.

Nighttime

Two-thirds of rapes and sexual assaults are committed between 6 P.M. and 6 A.M.

(See *Afternoons; Daytime; Mornings*)

North Carolina

Turn on your tarheels and flee. North Carolina is the buckle of the stroke belt, with twice the death rate from stroke as the rest of the country. The state is also the epicenter of prostate cancer deaths, and claims the nation's fifth highest bicycle rider mortality rate.

Nutmeg

A pinch here, a snort there... get by with a little help from your pantry.

Nutmeg can be a trip. The cooking spice, which contains elemicin, a compound related to mescaline, has been turning people on ever since the Crusades. All it takes is a lusty whiff or mouthful, and this is your brain on nutmeg: rapid heartbeat, constipation, dry mouth, bloodshot eyes, incoherent speech, and impaired motor function. A dealer lurks in every neighborhood; just say no.

O

Offices

Offices are calling in sick, and it's contagious.

Office buildings are hotbeds of contaminants, structures that hermetically seal in workers, who must toil among filthy air ducts, moldy ceiling tiles, formaldehyde-leaking floors, chemically cleaned furniture, asthma-causing insect poop, and ozone-emitting laser printers. Air circulation in the workaday tombs is ineffectual; air purification is lacking altogether.

The Occupational Safety and Health Administration shakes an accusing but impotent finger at airtight contemporary architecture, blaming it for "sick building syndrome," the headachy, red-eyed, sore-throated bundle of recurring symptoms suffered by millions of office workers.

(See *Photocopying*)

Olive Oil

The darling of the world of fats may not be the dietary holy grail after all. A study shows that olive oil, which is supposed to protect against heart disease, may not be up to the job. Wake Forest University lab mice were fed either diets containing saturated fat, like that in butter and meat, or polyunsaturated fat, found in vegetable oil, or olive oil's monounsaturated fat. The olive-oiled mice were more likely to develop atherosclerosis than the other fat-fed rodents. Researchers, in an American Heart Association publication, declare that linoleic acid-rich oils, such as corn and soybean, seem to protect against coronary disease more so than olive oil.

Online Investing

With one click, you could lose your assets but that's only one way to get cyberscrewed.

Once upon a time, it was your stockbroker who sweated out every twist and turn of the market, while you relaxed and clipped coupons. Nowadays, with online, no-broker investing, you're wired into a desktop pressure cooker, monitoring minute-by-minute every ulcer-making Wall Street blip, making blood pressure-raising sell-and-buy decisions—all by your greedy little self.

Going brokerless is more convenient and cheaper than hiring a stockbroker, but on-line investing, besides causing the jitters, is gulag lonely. There's no one around to offer nerve-soothing advice, to comfort when a portfolio sucks wind, or to help put financial losses into a less stressful, bigger-picture perspective.

Opera

People are wrong when they say that the opera isn't what it used to be. It is *what it used to be. That's what's wrong with it.* —Noël Coward

Wagner and road rage: words never before used in the same sentence. That is, until England's Royal Automobile Club warbled about the temper-riling hazards of driving while listening to music like the German composer's rousing "The Ride of the Valkyries," which the auto club alleges can pique a motorist's anger, increasing the likelihood of a wrathful crack-up. Some music therapists agree that up-tempo rhythms with more than sixty beats per minute are heart-rate increasing and nerve agitating. The safety experts sing the praises of calmer driving ditties, and suggest listening to tunes by Enya, or the soothing, "Blue Danube Waltz."

Please, let the fat lady sing.

Parakeets

Sounds a might peckish but a plumed pet can make you sick as a dog. Psittacosis, a disease transmitted to humans from birds of the parrot family, is spread by inhaling bird-dropping dust, which can remain infectious for weeks.

Now you know what the caged bird flings.

(See *Cats; Dogs; Hedgehogs; Lizards*)

Parsley

Shigellosis isn't a bop dance from the go-go sixties, but a diabolical food poisoning that KO'd hundreds of people a few years back after they munched on parsley. That batch of tarnished garnish was contaminated by fecal bacteria from the water source on the farm where it was grown, but restaurants also corrupt the curly vegetable by leaving it out at room temperature, which only tempts the growth of loathsome bacteria.

(See *Five Servings a Day*)

Party Favors

The National Injury Information Clearinghouse keeps track of the reasons why people arrive broken and wounded at hospital emergency rooms, and in its annual report, the federal government pooper has a category for party favors.

Revelers have choked on flung confetti, splintered ankles tripping over streamers, and shattered face parts with ill-aimed piñata bats.

Next shindig, nix the trinkets, unless you're in the running for the title of hostess with the mostest lawsuits.

Party Lights

The party host wanted his living room to have a hip club ambience so he replaced the light bulbs in his lamps with bulbs intended for use in reptile tanks. Groovy.

Amid the spectral glow, the lounge lizards almost danced their sight away. The morning after was a blur: the revelers woke with painful eye spasms that forced their eyelids shut. The *British Medical Journal* reports all were treated successfully, and strongly advises using party lights that emit visible wavelengths.

Paved Roads

It's an asphalt jungle out there. The *Internal Medical News* unearthed research findings indicating that dust from paved roads sets off skin reactions in one out of four Southern California study participants.

Peppermints

Peppermints don't do much for heartburn. Instead, the suckers stoke tummy-burning sensations by weakening the esophagus muscle that's supposed to close down the stomach and protect it against irritants.

Pass up the patties.

Percolated Coffee

The percolating combo of hot water and coffee grounds creates oils called terpenes, which can raise serum cholesterol levels. The longer the water and grounds mix it up, the more terpenes are produced. Drip for all the perks of the best joe.

Personal Computers

Working wounded.

Most people who spend hours hunched over computer keyboards will develop nerve damage in their upper limbs, neurophysiological studies have shown. Repetitive stress injuries—carpal tunnel syndrome (affecting the hands, wrists, arms, neck, upper back, and shoulders), lower back injuries, neck stiffness—now account for more than 60 percent of new cases of workplace illnesses.

Eyestrain, you strain, we all strain in front of computer screens, and what's to show for it? Blurred vision, sore eyes, and migraines. Seventy-five percent of workers who squint at computer monitors have eye and vision problems, cites the American Optometric Association. Our eyes just weren't meant to focus close-up all day. After peering at a screen for a long time, looking up is a muscular effort that can cause eye spasms and fuzzy vision. Darting from documents to screen, from screen to keyboard and back again, can induce a form of repetitive stress injury that requires a long recovery time.

Teach your children well. Physicians and physical therapists worry the lack of appropriate equipment and furniture, along with an absence of training in posture and keyboard techniques, will inevitably produce a flood of injuries. Kids are starting on the nerd track at very young ages, learning bad computer habits along the way. Adult-sized workstations force the little peckers into awkward positions. After observing elementary schoolers slumped at computer workstations, Cornell University researchers concluded that at least four in ten were at risk for serious injury.

Be somewhat of a Luddite; limit Junior's computer time and plunk him in front of the tube.

(See *Internet; Watching Television*)

Personal Stereos

Geezers aren't the only ones going deaf. An alarming number of people in their forties and fifties, teens as well, are saddled with noise-induced hearing loss. Listening to cranked-up, 113-decibel personal stereos for hours at a stretch isn't helping matters. If someone else toe taps to your solitary music, it's loud enough to do harm. Turn it down.

Photocopying

The practice of cloning make you sick? Your hives, runny nose, and headaches might be an allergic reaction to a photocopier's chemical fumes. Use the machine in a well-ventilated area to stop duplicating the irritating symptoms.

(See *Offices*)

Picking Your Nose

The indecorous practice of nosepicking can be calamitous. If a ransacking finger gouges the mucous membrane of your nasal passage, it could bring on an infection, which could travel to your brain and cause a blood clot.

Use a hankie, not your pinkie.

Playgrounds

They're not all fun and games. The majority of America's playgrounds are unfit for children, alerts the National Program for Playground Safety, an organization with cause for alarm: Playground injuries have more than doubled in the past two decades. In 1998, some 616,000 playground-injured children were treated in emergency departments and doctors' offices; as many as seventeen children die every year in playground mishaps.

Swings, monkey bars, jungle gyms, overhead ladders, rings, and slides are the main offenders, with falls making up 70 percent of the accidents. The American Academy of Orthopaedic Surgeons—the specialists who mend many of the playground-battered children—recommends that all recreation areas be equipped with shock-absorbing surfaces, with separate play areas for younger kids, rubber or plastic swings, lower-to-the-ground slides, and vigilant adult supervision.

(See *Sandboxes*)

Playing Rock and Roll

Karaoke 'til you drop.

After playing a head-bobbing, neck-twisting gig in 1998, funk king Rick James complained of dizziness and numbness on his right side. Two blood vessels had burst in the rocker's neck, causing him to suffer a debilitating stroke. Doctors call the rhythmic whiplashing "rock and roll neck," and serve notice to other rockers about the perilous head-banging movement.

(See *Making Music*)

Pogo Sticks

Pogo stick riders hop to emergency rooms with lacerated faces, broken teeth, shattered bones, and even severe head injuries.

Go and pogo no mo.

Popcorn

Popcorn's got this rep as a healthful low-cal, low-fat treat. Sure, as long as it's not coated with oozy butter, unsalted, and air-popped. So what if it tastes like Styrofoam? At least it's not an artery closer.

Americans do love their popcorn, putting away a total of 640 million pounds a year, with the king of pop the microwave variety. Oiled up, buttered, salted, sometimes sugared, and even sulfited, the quick snack's not even close to being nutritious.

Biting down on unpopped kernels—called "old maids" by the misogynistic popcorn industry because they're too dry to have any pop left—can shatter salary-draining dental work.

Come on into the lobby. Part of the ritual of moviegoing includes munching on popcorn, but now doctors warn of the risk of severe contact burns from some theaters' self-service hot-butter dispensers, set to skin-blazing temperatures of 212° F.

Pop culture hit a new low in North Carolina when a man, claiming to have laced movie popcorn with his dead aunt's ashes, demanded money from the theater chain to keep mum about the tainted concession. Arrested and charged with extortion, the seventy-seven-year-old weasel confessed to putting just charcoal (just charcoal?) in the popcorn of several theaters, admitting that Aunt Tessie wasn't even cremated. In a letter to theater execs, the jackash apologized to the "hundreds upon hundreds of thousands of movie patrons" who ate the "cannibal corn."

Popping Out of a Cake

Confess. You've had the life-long fantasy of springing from a five-layer rum cake, looking quite tasty yourself, to surprise your sweetie. But, don't wait too long to take the leap. When a stag-party stripper, who'd been nestled for hours inside an air-sealed pastry missed her cue, guests opened the cake to find her suffocated, none too poppin' fresh.

Posturing

When your jaw aches, slouching toward analgesics won't do you any good. Take a better stance. Slovenly posture creates muscle tension in the head, neck, or upper back, and can cause chronic mouth and jaw pain.

Potato Guns

Stop or I'll spud.

Made on a shoestring—plastic tubing, a lawn mower engine, batteries, and hairspray—potato guns propel their veggie ammo as far as 900 feet. The Saturday-night-blue-plate-specials can snap a 2x4 in half, and if you come eye-to-eye with one of these homespun sidearms, you're risking big trouble.

Case studies from the medical journal *Ophthalmology* prove the half-baked sidearms are very dangerous. A fourteen-year-old boy, shot in the face, suffered severe, life-threatening trauma; he lived but surgeons eventually removed his right eye. Another kid was luckier; doctors were able to repair his lacerated all-to-hell cornea.

The Bureau of Alcohol, Tobacco and Firearms doesn't acknowledge potato guns as firearms, but the American Academy of Ophthalmology argues that the weaponry is a definite safety threat.

Powdered Latex Gloves

With a couple of million patients picking up infections during their hospital stays, the latex-gloved hands of health care workers should be reassuring. Trouble is, a good whiff of the powder inside the latex gloves can cause powerful allergic reactions.

An estimated 8 percent of the nation's seven million health care workers suffer latex-related allergies, as do thousands of hospital patients. The powder in rubber gloves, which makes them easier to pull on and off, sends dust clouds of allergens into the air. Reactions range from itching and hives to breathing difficulties and even life-threatening shock. The Public Citizen Health Research Group has identified powdered latex gloves as a menace in hospitals and recommends a powder-free variety, which many health care facilities now use.

(See *Hospitals*)

Power Windows

A Department of Transportation study rolls out the statistic that hands, wrists, or fingers of nearly 500 people are fractured, crushed, dislocated, and otherwise abused annually by power windows in vehicles.

Prescriptions by Mail

Neither snow nor rain nor heat nor gloom of night...back up there. Copping prescription drugs over the Internet or through catalogues may save a trip to the pharmacy, but could have you dealing with endangered products.

Recent tests by U.S. Pharmacopeia showed that more than a quarter of mailed prescriptions, packed with temperature-recording devices, were subjected to temperatures of 100° F or higher; only 8 percent of the meds stayed at room temperature during shipping. Leaving prescription medications in mailboxes, especially during the summer months, might subject them to extreme heat, which could have deleterious effects on their efficacy, potency, and safety.

Produce Sections

Grocers no longer linger over produce sections, hose in hand, to douse wilted arugula with freshening water squirts. Nowadays, a fine mist from an automated, overhead sprinkling system does the wet work. You're much safer with the hoser. The spritzes from a Louisiana supermarket's produce section caused a major outbreak of the highly infectious Legionnaire's disease. Two grocery shoppers died and scores were sickened from breathing the bacteria-laden drizzle.

Public Speaking

The fear of public speaking is by far the most prevalent social anxiety. Americans are more spooked about speaking to a group of people than they are of going to the dentist, of flying, of creepy-crawly spiders, or of the dark of night. Some dread it even more than the prospect of their own death.

A medical study at East Tennessee State University shows that stage fright could mean a final curtain call. Heart patients with clogged blood vessels underwent a stress test while giving five-minute speeches before an audience. On average, the speakers' blood pressures soared by some 40 points; in half of the patients, sections of the left ventricle muscle beat erratically, a frightening indication that the heart isn't receiving enough oxygen. About four years later, a follow-up study found that the ones who suffered the scary irregular heartbeats were three times more likely to have died of heart disease than the less jittery speakers. Public speaking didn't kill them, but rather their reactions to the type of stress it generated.

Having pals in an audience may ease your public speaking willies but those friendly faces won't do much for your performance, claims the *Journal of Personality and Social Psychology*. Recent studies show that sympathetic, supportive spectators only make public speakers think they're doing okay when actually they contribute to a bad performance, whereas neutral observers, whose opinions the performers didn't care about, or unfavorable audiences actually improved performances.

Pumping Iron

Only dumbbells lift weights while taking antibiotics. Germ-fighting medications commonly used to treat urinary tract, bronchial, or intestinal infections have been linked to more than 100 cases of tendonitis and tendon ruptures.

Body parts most at jeopardy are the Achilles tendons, knees, quads, and rotator cuffs. Doctors say finish off the meds, then head for the weight room.

Pumpkin Carving

It's somewhat ghoulish but every October doctors must reach in their healing bag of tricks to treat pumpkin carvers' knife-gouged hands for puncture wounds and lacerations. Take your time and closely supervise any wee goblins.

(See *Halloween*)

Quitting Smoking

London's Institute of Psychiatry discloses that nicotine withdrawal can make smokers goofy, disoriented, and confused (so what's new?). More nonfatal industrial accidents occur on the Wednesday of England's No-Smoking Day (the British version of the Great American Smokeout) than on the Wednesday before or the Wednesday after the smoke-free day. Blimey. The shrinks advocate using a nicotine replacement, like the patch or gum, before slamming the brakes on the disgusting habit.

Racquet Sports

Where's the love?

The body's no match for racquet sports' pivoting, slamming, and snapping motions—tennis, racquetball, squash, and badminton lay players up with abrasions, lacerations, rips, strains, sprains, blisters, corns, and calluses.

Racquet-sport balls can easily travel faster than 100 mph. Wear goggles made with polycarbonate to protect your eyes (hospital emergency rooms treat nearly 40,000 sports eye injuries every year) from the rocketing missiles and from getting a hurtful racquet rap.

Rain

Coming in from it is the easy part. Sudden drops in barometric pressure that cause sprinkles can give you a headache, weather you like it or not.

Raw Milk

Got germs? Unpasteurized milk does, scoundrels like salmonella, listeria, and brucellosis, at-the-ready to turn a mustache-smile upside down. From 1973 to 1992 in the United States, outbreaks of diseases associated with raw milk were reported—forty-five of them—more than enough for medical types to udder a call for a ban of its sale.

Recliner Chairs

Hey, all you lazy boys: Keep kids away from recliner chairs. Health Canada and the Consumer Product Safety Commission report injuries and suffocation deaths from children trapped in the opening between the comfy chair and its leg rest. Voluntary standards adopted by the American Furniture Manufacturers Association now prohibit the child-snaring gap in new models to be wider than 5 inches. Older chairs with large openings should be adjusted or thrown out.

(See *Yard Sales*)

Red Food

Dare you to eat a bug. Aw, you win, big time.

Don't gag, but you've probably swallowed thousands of tiny beetles, called cochineals. Raised in Central and South America and harvested by the billions, the critters are squished to extract carmine, a dye that's been used ever since the Aztecs to turn food, cosmetics, and textiles varying shades of red.

Hundreds of foods and drinks, including frozen cherry treats, festive Christmas pasta, grape-flavored gum, ruby-tinted aperitifs, and fruity yogurts derive their color from the extract of cochineals, the only bug approved for consumption by the FDA. Because the watchdog agency considers it a natural additive, the coloring isn't subjected to strict regulations as are synthetic dyes. Carmine-colored food and drinks simply have to be labeled "color added" or "artificial color."

Fine, who honestly wants to see "bugs" on a bottle of pop? The person allergic to carmine for one. Using Red Scare tactics, Dr. James L. Baldwin warns that carmine can induce mild hives and itchy skin, and in some cases, even life-threatening anaphylactic shock. The University of Michigan allergist, while not advocating a ban of the colorant, is keen on making physicians and consumers more aware of possible sensitivities to the dye, and urges the FDA to at least require carmine to be listed on food labels.

(See *Maraschino Cherries*)

Red Kidney Beans

Oh poot! There's more to worry about than breaking wind after a meal of red kidney beans. A toxic agent (phytohaemagglutinin, if you must know) is found in many kinds of beans, with the highest concentration in red kidney beans. Eaten raw or undercooked, the beans are wicked, causing extreme nausea, profuse vomiting, and diarrhea.

Raw-bean salads were the culprits in several recent outbreaks of red kidney bean poisoning. Guilty, too, have been slow-cooking crock pots; heat kills the legume toxin, and cooking temperatures of the pokey appliances often aren't anywhere hot enough to neutralize the virulent pathogen. Undercooked red kidney beans are even more sickening than raw ones because just a little heat—about 80° F—increases their toxicity fivefold.

Foodies recommend that red kidney beans be soaked in water for 5 hours, then boiled in fresh water for at least 10 minutes before cooking at 160° F.

(See *Slow Cookers*)

Refrigerator Magnets

Fridge magnets attract trouble. Little kids swallow them; adults get facial cuts and eye lacerations after sideswiping the appliance decorations. Ice the kitsch.

Religion

Religious people are more inclined to be overweight than the less reverent, so sayeth a Purdue University study that was published, chapter and verse, in the *Review of Religious Research.*

Even though gluttony is one of the seven deadly sins, perhaps the more spiritual-minded assign God's dictate "Go forth and multiply" to an ever-spreading waistline. Or maybe it's as Purdue's investigators theorize: Religious groups are far more accepting of their chubby brethren than is our cellulite-despising society as a whole.

The research also bears witness that pulpits, while preaching moderation in most aspects of daily living, may not sermonize about the evils lurking in devil's food cake.

Remote Controls

Surf bored? Could be an allergy to the latex remote control. Millions of people respond badly to rubber-based products—

some have mild physical reactions, while others suffer life-threatening breathing difficulties. Get off your duff and change the channel.

(See *Watching Television*)

Renting

2 br, 1 bth, no vu, neuroses incl.

Renters are an anxious and depressed lot, deposits the medical journal *The Lancet*. Investigative interviews of nearly 10,000 British residents by the University of Wales College of Medicine compared the psychological profiles of renters to those of home-owners. People who rent were more likely to suffer from neurotic disorders, such as anxiety and depression.

What's up? The Welsh researchers assumed that renters have lower incomes than mortgage holders, which makes them feel excluded from society, which creates more difficulties and anxieties in dealing with stressful events.

Restaurant Meats

Fittingly enough, an outfit called the Lawrence Livermore National Laboratory sends up smoke signals about restaurant-cooked meats—burgers, steaks, and pork ribs—claiming they're loaded with more cancer-causing compounds (as much as ten times higher) than are meats cooked at fast-food joints.

Heterocyclic amines (a mouthful for animal carcinogens that many scientists believe contribute to people cancer) are formed during long cooking times at hot temperatures. Livermore chemists profess that fast-food prep is, duh, quicker and at lower temps than that of most regular restaurants; therefore, the speedy cooking method doesn't support the formation of the sinister compounds.

You deserve a big break. Drive on through.

Retail Sales Jobs

HELP wanted.

Behind a counter or peddling door-to-door, staying alive may be the hardest sell of all. The estimated 22 million U.S. employees in retail sales are more likely to be violently killed on the job than are other people in the workforce.

Between 1992 and 1996, roughly 3 retail workers per 100,000 died on the job, reports the Department of Labor, which attributes the wholesale slaughter to violence (70 percent) and to motor vehicle accidents (19 percent). Liquor store employees have the highest fatality rates (almost exclusively from homicide), followed by grocery store employees, and automotive suppliers and dealers.

Riverside, California

The corridor between Riverside and San Bernardino claims title to being tops in the nation for fatalities attributed to aggressive driving. The Surface Transportation Policy Project reports that belligerent-driving deaths are much higher in communities with uncontrolled sprawl, high-speed roads, and endless strip malls—exactly the kind of landscape that begs a driver to slow down and take in the scenery.

Rock Concerts

Rock of ages.

The "Fleetwood Mac Attack," as dubbed by Dr. Stuart W. Rosenbush in *The Journal of the American Medical Association,* could affect more and more rock concertgoers. Take the case of the middle-aged coronary bypass patient who almost stopped thinking about tomorrow during a Fleetwood Mac concert. About an hour into the show, the chest of the recuperating man started to hurt, so he nixed the concert and left. His cardiologist's diagnosis:

not-so-good-vibrations from the intensely loud onstage music. Dr. Rosenbush says: "As the baby boomer generation, who grew up with booming rock music (myself included), enters the age group in which coronary artery bypass surgery becomes more prevalent, this syndrome potentially could become more frequent."

Rock on, but protect your eyes and ears, life and limbs. The average rock concert blasts music at 120 decibels, plenty loud enough to damage hearing. During the 1996 Lollapalooza tour the nonprofit organization Hearing Awareness and Education for Rockers distributed 60,000 earplugs. At another concert, goggles would have been nice for the seventeen-year-old girl hit in the eye with a tossed-from-the-stage CD that sliced her cornea.

It's a hard rock life. Although the number of deaths in 1998 at musical venues worldwide dropped by more than half from the decade-high nineteen in 1997, five times as many people got hurt from crushing crowd surges, mosh pits, fires, shootings, stabbings, and drownings. Paul Wertheimer of the Chicago-based safety consulting firm Crowd Management Strategies blames the mayhem on poor security, festival seating, and lousy planning. Venting in the *Fort Worth Star-Telegram*, Wertheimer grouses: "We still have no standard for concert safety. The industry doesn't treat people in a safe, reasonable manner. Kids hyped about seeing their favorite band don't think about it." Tomorrow or otherwise.

(See *Classical Performances; Earplugs; Gospel Concerts; Slam Dancing; Underwire Bras*)

Roses

By any other name, it's sporotrichosis. The fungal disease you catch from roses is usually transmitted through small thorn cuts on your hands. Infecting the skin and lymph nodes, sporotrichosis causes an ugly rash and skin lesions. Avoid pricks of all kinds. Wear garden gloves.

Runways

There's something awfully LAX at U.S. airports. "Runway incursions," what the aviation industry calls near-misses during takeoffs and landings, are increasing—325 of the almost-disasters occurred in 1998, up 11 percent from the year before. The largest share of the goof-ups—some 183 incidents—were caused by pilot error.

Los Angeles International Airport had the most runway incursions in 1998, with close calls at Lambert Field in St. Louis and Newark International Airport trailing close behind.

Salad Mixes

Mesclun around with unwashed greens is chancy. Store-bought salad mixes can harbor the disease-causing *E. coli* 0157:H7. Don't risk it. Rinse all salad fixings well under cold running water.

Sandboxes

All castles should house an infirmary. Odious germs, like staphylococcus and the dreaded *E. coli*, wallow in sandboxes, on deck to slither into kids' scrapes and cuts.

(See *Playgrounds*)

Saturdays

It's the loneliest night of the week, except at the morgue. More fatal motor-vehicle accidents happen on Saturdays than on any other day of the week, with the bumper crop of crashes occurring between 4 P.M. and 4 A.M.

(See *Mondays; Fridays; Weekends*)

Scary Movies

Psycho cross dressers, flesh-ripping sharks, and machete madmen are fearsome screen fun, but some moviegoers don't have the fright stuff.

In a terror-effect study, 26 percent of surveyed college students said they suffered long-term emotional or behavioral problems from watching scary movies they saw as a child or teenager, and about a third admitted they still had the heebie-jeebies more than a year later. The younger the subjects were when they saw a disturbing flick, the longer they were troubled by it.

(See *Soundtracks*)

Seafood

Is it only a fishwives' tale that 113,000 cases of seafood poisoning strike Americans every year? Nope, it's fact. Most of the sea sick suffer from the Norwalk virus (about 100,000), but tuna and mackerel can serve up throat-swelling, skin-rashing scombroid poisoning, and grouper and barracuda might dish out ciguetera, a devastating neurotoxin. Fish eaters have also been infected with parasites (the anisakis worm bores holes in an eater's gut, excretes waste from its face, and before it finally dies in a week or so, can cause unbearable pain), tapeworm larvae, and mad-fish disease.

It's a raw deal, but uncooked oysters are blamed for more serious illnesses than any other seafood. The problems start when the tasty troublemakers loll in polluted waters, absorbing, along with nutrients, harmful bacteria and viruses through their shells.

In many mollusk harvesting areas, the greatest hazard has nothing to do with funky water but with a sneaky bacteria that can turn malicious. *Vibrio vulnificus*—undetectable by sight, smell, or taste—is commonly found in Gulf of Mexico oysters and, while not a threat to most healthy people, can cause sudden chills, fever, gastric upset, blood poisoning, and even death in some oyster eaters who have medical conditions, like liver disease, alcoholism, weakened immune systems, and hepatitis. An average of ten people a year die from eating raw Gulf oysters.

Thoroughly cooking seafood knocks out *Vibrio vulnificus* and the Norwalk virus; parasites are snuffed out by freezing as well as heat, which, unfortunately, has no effect on ciguetera or scombroid toxins.

(See *Fishing*)

Shadowy Streets

Dark canyons of cityscapes may contribute to higher breast cancer rates of women living in large Northern cities. Unlike sun-drenched Southern women, the urban dwellers are robbed of vitamin D–enriched sunlight that's blocked by crammed-together tall buildings.

Studying eighty-seven regions around the country, scientists from the University of California at San Diego turned up a close relationship between breast cancer death rates and the amount of solar radiation that reached the ground, speculating that vitamin D inhibits the development of breast cancer. While theorizing about the sunny side of the street, the researchers caution women about trying to prevent breast cancer with excessive exposure to sun only to develop melanoma, the deadly skin cancer.

(See *Sunlight*)

Shoes

Your dogs are howling, and it's probably that your shoes are too tight, too high, or too small. If you're ill-shod, before you step off this planet, you're likely to have some kind of foot problem—bunions, corns, calluses, hammertoes, or fungus.

Shoes can trip you up, too; more than 75,000 people hot-footed it to emergency rooms from shoe-related accidents in 1997. High heels cause many tumbles, but even the most practical footwear can be problematic, especially if you've been around the block a few times. A survey of older patients at the Orthopedic Hospital in Los Angeles noted that a quarter of the seniors had been wearing flat, sturdy shoes when they fell and couldn't get up.

Revive your sole. Go barefoot.

(See *Socks; Stiletto Heels; Wearing Clothes*)

Shopping Carts

Ever see a parent strap a child into a shopping cart? Probably not. And, it's a shame. Safety belts are on shopping carts for a good reason: to keep kids from standing up in and falling out of the narrow-based, top-heavy buggies.

About 22,000 bruised and mauled kids, some with severe lacerations and closed head injuries, wheel into emergency rooms every year. Buckle up.

Shortness

Size matters.

Men under 5 feet, 7 inches have more heart attacks than the guys they look up to. A study of males by Brigham and Women's Hospital and the Harvard Medical School calculated a 3 percent decrease in the risk of heart attack for every inch of height. The scientists speculate that runts are shortchanged because they have narrower arteries and weaker lungs, both physiological links to an increased chance of heart disease. Other research confirms that short men are given to be obese, poor, heavy smokers, and prone to heart disease and stroke (one in five, compared to only one in ten for the tall men).

(See *Tallness*)

Short Skirts

Nothing mini about the skin-cancer dangers posed by the sun. Women are more likely than men to develop melanoma on their legs. Don't hem and haw about this merciless form of skin cancer. Baste your exposed body parts with lots o' sunscreen boasting a high SPF factor.

(See *Sunlight; Sunscreen*)

Singing in the Choir

With peak sound levels of more than 110 decibels (jackhammer loud), choirs can be holy terrors on singers' hearing. The University of Vienna Medical School diagnosed hearing impairments among members of a large choir and conjectured that the do-re-mi-fa-*so*-loud singing increased the fluid pressure in the singers' inner ears, which caused the hearing loss.

Sixteen-Year-Old Drivers

Sweet sixteen and never been dissed. Well, now's the time.

Teens far exceed all other age groups in terms of per capita deaths as both drivers and passengers, with sixteen-year-olds owning the biggest risk. According to the Insurance Institute for Highway Safety, among teen drivers, sixteen-year-olds have, by far, the highest rate of teenage passenger deaths in their vehicles per licensed driver and per mile driven.

(See *Car Phones*)

Ski Wax

Breathing in the fumes from melted ski wax can mess up your lungs. The wax itself is safe but the heating process emits dangerous fluorocarbons. Swiss researchers, alarmed about a reported

300 cases of lung toxicity, caution skiers to melt wax in open or ventilated areas.

Slam Dancing

Kibosh the mosh.

Taking a slam to the chest could cancel your dance card, permanently. Doctors call it *commotio cordis,* a concussion to the heart. Here's what happens: As the heart beats, there's an ever-so fleeting moment when its electrical cycle is resetting, gearing up for the next contraction. If, precisely in that fraction of a second, a body blow is delivered on just the right place on the chest, the heart stutters and breaks its rhythmic, blood-pumping lub dub lub dub. The heart, out of sync and quivering, beats no more.

Commotio cordis happens on the playing fields of soccer, hockey, and baseball as well as in mosh pits. More than twenty-five athletes have been reported killed from a blunt blow to the chest.

Slam Dunks

In your hoop dreams.

The American Dental Association gives the high sign: Slam dunking a basketball could result in the net loss of a few molars. Lowering the backboard, or taking flying leaps off raised platforms makes it easier for kids to emulate the NBA's tall men in short pants, but the rim-colliding young air Jordans are fast breaking out teeth. One ten-year-old hoopster caught his teeth in a metal-chain net, ripping out one tooth and fracturing three others.

Advice from the ADA: No rim hanging, and keep both feet near the ground, something the pros should entertain.

Sleep

Lullaby and, good night! Americans are grinding their teeth in epidemic proportions. The nocturnal habit can be destructive, causing headaches, sore jaws, and permanent tooth damage. The usual suspect: stress. Train your jaw muscles to relax during the day, don't chew gum or pencils that will accustom the muscles to clench, and cut back on caffeinated food and drinks that may create tension.

(See *Napping; Sleepless Nights; Snoring*)

Sleeping Bags

Snooze-alarm.

At least twenty sleeping-bag-abused people went to the hospital in 1998 with head injuries and broken bones caused by trips over the roll-up beds, and lacerations from fishhooks that were hidden in the padding. One sad sack was treated for penile bruises after a sleeping-bag zipper snafu.

(See *Camping*)

Sleepless Nights

Grab some shuteye. Spending a sleepless night may lead to heart attacks and strokes the next morning, allege Italian researchers, whose data show higher blood pressures and heart rates on the mornings after patients were deprived of sleep, which could increase the risk, especially for hypertensive people, for heart damage and cardiovascular disease.

(See *Sleep*)

Slow Cookers

Hurry up. Slow cookers can get you in a crock of trouble. Food that isn't prepared at high enough temperatures can be bacteria breeders. The FDA advises cranking up the dial to at least 160° F to bump off the brazen germs.

The Consumer Product Safety Commission stews about the cooking device as well, dismayed about the burns and lacerations caused by the pokey pots: Slow cookers have exploded, spewing skin-scalding food and liquids; too-heavy-to-hold lids have broken many a foot bone.

Fast food does have its merits.

(See *Red Kidney Beans*)

Small Heads

Bigger is better when it comes to a noggin. Small head circumference has been linked with an increased risk of Alzheimer's disease. Measuring 649 heads, researchers determined that the people with the smallest forehead size were two to three times more likely to be demented than those with the largest heads. The 1997 study, published in the journal *Neurology*, speculates that because people with bonsai-sized heads have less "reserve," they were more susceptible to dementia when Alzheimer's occurs.

Sneezes

Don't eschew an achoo...let 'er rip. Snuffing a sneeze might damage an eardrum or blow out a blood vessel in your head.

Snoring

Now I lay me down to sleep. I pray the Lord I don't snore. You better pray: All that grunting and snorting just might kill you, unless your bedmate offs you first.

Other than being a nightmare for the snoree, snooze-time

racket is pretty harmless, unless it signals sleep apnea, a disorder that makes snorers literally stop breathing, sometimes for as long as a minute, and as often as 300 times a night.

Researching the dangers of snoring and sleep apnea, a wide-awake team from the University of California at Los Angeles School of Dentistry nosed out the fact that a snorer's tongue falls back into the throat, blocking the airway. This results in a fitful struggle to breathe, causing snorting commotion and a rise in blood pressure, which in turn, damages the inner walls of the carotid arteries in the neck. Cholesterol gloms to these injured sites and prevents blood from flowing to the brain. The result can be a massive stroke. Much better to endure a sharp elbow to the ribs.

The SNORP Snoring Survey reveals that 71 percent of U.S. households claim a snorer, including 9 percent that boast of a log-sawing pet. About 28 percent admit that their beloved's snoring sounds like a buzz saw, while others likened the nocturnal sounds to a rumbling train, a jackhammer, and a pig. Sweet dreams.

(See *Fat Necks*)

Soap Operas

You'd have to be in another world not to know that soap operas portray a distorted view of passion and romance. Now, the *British Medical Journal,* a guiding light of the medical profession, has published an article about the daytime serials' depiction of child-birth and death.

Dr. Sarah Clement analyzed ninety-two TV childbirth scenarios (which would take way too many days of our lives to view) and reports that after an unrealistically short labor, the young and the restless mothers, without benefit of general hospitals, unexpectedly delivered their babies in unusual places, for instance, on a sunset beach. With only one life to live, the fictional moms had unrealistically high numbers of complications and death; of the ninety-two show-biz births, four infants and one mother died, another five newborns and four mothers developed life-threatening (but quite theatrical, one may assume) situations. As the real world turns, the death rate of all our children is much lower.

Other researchers found the death rates of British soap opera characters to be higher than for any real-life occupation, with the daytimers three times as likely to croak from violent causes than is the general population. All this high drama distorts the reality of birth and death, health and illness, Dr. Clement warns, which could negatively affect viewers' behavior.

Socks

A pair of socks can be a singular disaster. E.R.s treat hundreds of sock-wearing accident victims who have slipped and taken bad spills. Ignore the next bootie call.

(See *Shoes; Wearing Clothes*)

Soundtracks

No! Stop! Don't go into the woods! Can't you hear the spooky music?!?

Tension-building movie soundtracks frighten people more than watching the bloody rampage of a chain saw massacre. It's the musical allusion of horror and gore, the hell-of-a-note, spine-tingling chords suggesting a closeted bogeyman or leg-shredding shark that send the most shivers down our spines, claims the *Journal of General Psychology.*

(See *Scary Movies*)

Sour Candies

Acidic sour candies erode tooth enamel. Suck sweeter.

The South

Southerners are probably not more hospitable than New Englanders are; they are simply more willing to remind you of the fact that they are being hospitable. —Ray L. Birdwhistell

Watch your back; the South may rise again; its murder rate sure has. Dixie has the highest murder rate in the country, almost double that of the Northeast. The crimes, like the region itself, are down-home and friendly, with more often than not, killer and victim acquainted somehow—barroom brawls, lovers' spats, and friendly quarrels that escalate into hard-hearted affairs.

Down yonder, people are also at greater peril of having a chronic disease, twangs Atlanta's Centers for Disease Control and Prevention. Binge drinking, which is linked to driving while intoxicated, is higher among Southerners, of whom a high proportion are smokers and who are way-too-many-grits-plumper than the national average. In some parts of the South, in the so-called stroke belt, the death risk from the cardiovascular accident is twice as high as the national average.

Y'all come back.

Soy

Sounds nuts, but an excellent source of protein can also be a killer. Soy, mixed in some breads, hamburgers, sausages, and other meat products, is a botanical relation of the peanut, and like its cuz, has caused severe food-allergy attacks, as well as fatalities.

Spain

Eurotrash that holiday to Spain. The medical journal *Eurosurveillance* reports that Spain leads thirty-eight other countries in the number of tourist-contracted cases of the often-fatal Legionnaire's disease. In fairness, the numbers reflect Spain's lure to more visitors; the rate of Legionnaire's infection among visitors to the Mediterranean country was found to be no higher than that among travelers to other countries. But the problem is serious enough that Spain's tour operators are held liable if they knowingly place clients in hotels that may be a source of infection.

Sports Drinks

It's the pause that decays. A parched mouth leaves your tooth enamel more vulnerable to attack by sugar and acid. Like fruit juices and sodas, sports drinks can be high in both ingredients. Try sipping the high-energy beverages icy cold (acids work slower at cooler temps) through a straw to keep your pearlies white.

Spring

Springtime is total misery for the 35 million Americans allergic to pollinating trees and grasses, which could serve to explain why, traditionally, more people kill themselves during the blooming season than any other time of year, although recently, summer suicide rates have been topping spring's.

Winter's dreariness would seem to be the likely nudge to push the suicide-inclined to the brink, but psychologists allege that the cold interval serves as a societal glue. This we're-all-in-the-gloom-together vanishes when warm weather arrives. By then, the already lonely and isolated, watching all the happy, hand-holding, strolling-about friends and lovers, become even more despondent. Maybe they should spring for a good therapist.

(See *Autumn; Summer; Therapy; Winter*)

Squirrels

A degenerative brain condition has been linked to eating squirrel brains. Yes, squirrel brains. The mind-blowing rodent ingredients

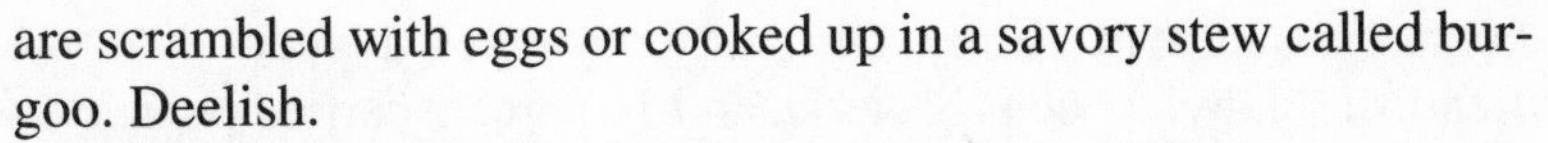

are scrambled with eggs or cooked up in a savory stew called burgoo. Deelish.

In Kentucky, where a million squirrels are killed every year, cases of Creutzfeldt-Jakob disease, a disorder similar to mad cow disease, have been diagnosed.

Tofu omelet for two?

(See *Kentucky*)

Stemming Tears

Go ahead and have a bawl.

A soggy sob will do you good. In fact, it's a crying shame if you bottle up unhappy emotions. Turning on the water works protects your body from all kinds of stress-related, heart-weakening chemicals.

(See *Crying*)

Stethoscopes

Tell your doctor to stick that stethoscope in his ear.

Every year, about 2 million hospital patients pick up infections that are caused by bacterial villains—some of the very same germs that swarm on stethoscopes, according to University of Michigan medical school research that tested forty of the heart-listening instruments. All the stethoscopes were contaminated; eleven different species of bacteria could be identified, including staphylococcus, a spiteful bug that causes pneumonia, meningitis, boils, and toxic shock. Next checkup, have an R.N. listen to your ticker since the investigation determined nurses' stethoscopes had significantly fewer bacteria colonies than did physicians'.

Still think cleanliness is next to doctorliness? Don't ask your physician to put it in writing; her pen's probably cruddy with germs, as were the doctors' ballpoints tested at the Salzburg General Hospital in Austria. Fifteen different species of bacteria were isolated on the writing instruments, with 93 percent of the pens contaminated with some kind of cootie; 71 percent had the fiendish staphylococcus bacteria, and 14 percent carried penicillin-resistant bugs. Have your doc phone in your next prescription.

Researchers in both studies admit there's no evidence that the pens and stethoscopes made anyone sick, but did recommend frequent swipes with germ-killing alcohol. Good medicine.

(See *Doctors' Writing; Hospitals*)

Stiff Palms

Your surgeon reads your palms. Do you: (1) alert the medical society, (2) hire a malpractice attorney, (3) try and make a good impression?

Go with 3. If your hands can't flatten out to create a complete palm print, it could indicate that during surgery the joints in your neck will be too rigid for anesthesiologists to position your head so a breathing tube can be easily slipped down your throat.

Of the 83 surgical patients whose palms were inked at the Yale University School of Medicine, forty-eight produced incomplete impressions, of whom, during an operation, nearly half had difficult intubations. Doctors had no trouble inserting the breathing tube in patients with whole palm prints.

Stiletto Heels

For a sexier look, fashion slaves have strapped on 5-inch stiletto heels since the shoes made their runway debut in the 1950s. Teetering on the high-altitude footwear reconfigures the body's silhouette by pushing the breasts and pelvis forward, accentuating the lower-back curve and tightening the calves. Seductive, yes, but stilettos also put pressure on the ball of the foot, squish toes together, and tilt the spine. It's hell on heels.

Called "limousine shoes" on the assumption that those who wear them never have to walk anywhere, stiletto heels have been cited as the cause of hammertoes, tendonitis, torn knee cartilage, herniated discs, ankle sprains, stress fractures, and chronic back pain.

In the style section of the *New York Times*, designer Manolo Blahnik, the high priest of the stiletto, scoffs at the medical concerns: "People simply walk different in high heels. Shall I call it suggestive? Shall I call it sensuous?"

Shall I call an ambulance?

(See *Shoes*)

Stone Floors

Year of the wheeze. Wealthy Chinese are mad for it; stone floors, furniture, sculpture, and fittings signal prosperity in the Far East, but the Bedrock décor has garnered less than glowing reviews. A Chinese news agency reports that radon, the radioactive gas released by granite and other stones, can cause lung cancer if inhaled in excessive amounts, and cites a survey finding that 27 percent of Chinese stone products failed radiation emission safety tests, with some decorative sculptures releasing five times the safe level of radiation. Yabba-dabba-don't.

Stools

The 1997 tally of the stool-injured treated at hospital emergency rooms was rung up by the Consumer Product Safety Commission; close to 14,500 clumsy climbers hobbled in with cut, bruised, and fractured body parts from falling off a stepped perch.

Avoid being part of the stool sample next year: Mount with care.

St. Patrick's Day

More alcohol-related traffic deaths occur on March 17 than on any other day of the year. Nearly 63 percent of the smashups on the holiday that honors a Christian monk are caused by the blarney-stoned.

Erin go figure.

Street Food

Salmonella on a stick.

Many push carts, toting tubs of raw meat and poultry, roasted animal parts, and eggs often left unchilled or unheated for hours, purvey a veritable smorgasbord of germs. Bacteria multiplies whenever food—uncooked or fully done—sits out at temps less than 140° F.

When's the last time you watched a vendor wash his hands or utensils? No soap and water means hepatitis A, fecal coliform, and staphylococcus could be regular items on the menu.

Curbside cuisine should hit the road.

Stress Tests

A good way to find out if you've got heart disease is to drop dead of cardiac arrest during a stress test. It's happened (although rarely). Get your heart checked out under the watchful gaze of a cardiologist, not a personal trainer at your health club.

Strong Hands

People with vigorous grips have greater odds of developing arthritis in their finger joints. Research published in *Arthritis and Rheumatism* shows that powerful hand muscles may exert excessive and debilitating force on the joints.

(See *Weak Hands*)

Stuffed Animals

House mites often infest cuddly toys. The scavenging little buggers might decide to abandon Winnie the Pooh to take refuge on your flaky, but to them, oh-so-tasty scalp. Nesting in your hair, the mites deposit poop proteins and, if you're prone to asthma, the fecal pellets could set off an attack.

Shampoo your beanie, baby.

Sugar Cane

Mesothelioma, a cancer associated most often with asbestos, is also linked to sugar cane, discloses the refined *British Medical Journal*.

Sugar-Free Gum

Look Ma, no cav . . . uh oh, be right back. Chewing scads of sugarless gum can give you the runs. The sugar-substituting chemicals—hexitol, sorbitol, and mannitol—pass into the small intestine and colon and tell your bowels to get a move on.

(See *Chewing Gum*)

Summer

Summer's a bummer.

For some people, the skin-torching, melanoma-making season is a fun bake-off time, but for others, the months only spark melancholy. Summer depression is a version of seasonal affective disorder, or SAD, which usually strikes during winter's melancholy sunless days, and is thought to be one of the reasons for the increase in hot-weather violent crimes, especially rape.

People with the summertime blues will get even SADder

because the season's getting hotter and stickier. In the next century, scientists expect a two- to six-degree increase in global temperature, with more frequent summer heat waves, especially steamy nights and crop-wilting droughts. The superheat's already on: The number of hot spells from 1949 to 1995 increased a blistering 88 percent, and medical scientists are sending an SOS about the health perils of extended periods of searing heat and humidity, nodding to the July 1995 Chicago sizzler that killed more than 600 people and sent 3,300 others swooning to emergency rooms. The summer of 1999 was no sissy either, a blazer responsible for more than 200 deaths.

Summertime and the livin' is queasy. It's not the heat, it's the eats. Grilled salmonella, barbecued *E. coli*, and broiled listeria are all too often served up at summer cookouts on account of undercooked meats, gone-bad potato salad, and unwashed, picnic-dirtied hands.

(See *August; Autumn; July; Spring; Winter*)

Sunglasses

Look on the dark side.

Blue, red, or orange sunglass lenses can obscure traffic signals or the flashing lights of emergency vehicles. Choose gray, brown, or green tints, with 100 percent UVA/UVB absorption. Non-UV shades, even with a dark tint, can be worse for your eyes than going without sunglasses since they cause pupils to dilate, allowing even more radiation to strike the eyeballs.

Sunlight

With profound apologies to Noël Coward, it's Yanks who go out in the noonday sun, with the mad dog notion they don't need protection from its torrid cancer-causing rays. The growing incidence of melanoma in America proves it. The virulent skin cancer, linked directly to the sun's ultraviolet radiation (as are basal-cell carcinomas), is rising faster than almost any other cancer.

The statistics are grim: In 1999, about 42,000 people were diagnosed with malignant melanoma; 9,200 died from it. It's the most common cancer among women between the ages of twenty-five and twenty-nine; and the second most prevalent, after breast cancer, among women between thirty and thirty-four. Melanoma is remorseless: Responsible for only 4 percent of all skin cancers, it accounts for 79 percent of skin cancer deaths. No one's immune, but the fair-skinned and light-eyed are at greater risk.

Eyes take a brutal hit from the cruel light, too. Exposure to ultraviolet B rays increases the risk of cataracts, a clouding of the clear lenses. Wear shades, but no need to waste a paycheck when you buy a pair; just be sure they're UV absorbent.

Do what the American Academy of Dermatology suggests: Avoid prolonged sun exposure, especially between 10 A.M. and 3 P.M.. Year-round (even on cloudy days), thickly apply (and do it often) sunscreen with an SPF of 15 or higher; wear wide-brimmed hats and long sleeves; protect your next of skin—sun exposure early in life may result in cancer decades later, so keep kids well protected; and give your entire body a good once-over regularly to check for changes that may occur in your skin.

(See *Short Skirts; Summer; Sunglasses; Sunscreen; Tanning Beds; Winter*)

Sunscreen

Sunscreen is taking heat from some scientists who caution that it may not keep you from getting melanoma, and that using it may actually increase the risk of the deadly skin cancer.

It seems wacky, but over the last twenty-five years as the use of sunscreen has become more common, the incidence of melanoma has risen sharply. Research at Memorial Sloan-Kettering Cancer Center in New York suggests that sunscreens, while preventing sunburn, give people a false sense of security, making them feel they can indulge in more sun time. *The Journal of the National Cancer Institute* reports corroborating evidence that sunbathers "should be warned against the danger that using a sunscreen may inadvertently prolong recreational sun exposure."

Do your best not to be counted among the million Americans diagnosed with skin cancer every year. Thwart the beams every way you can. Remember "Slip, Slop, Slap"—Australia's alliterative anti–skin cancer campaign slogan: *Slip* on a long-sleeved shirt, *Slop* on some SPF 15 or higher sunscreen, and *Slap* on a hat.

(See *Summer; Sunlight; Tanning Beds; Winter*)

Sweethearts

Love hurts. How romantic is it that 17 percent of all people and more than a third of the women who limp to emergency rooms with violence-inflicted injuries are there courtesy of a former or current spouse, boyfriend, or girlfriend? By some estimates, 4 million American women are seriously assaulted every year by an intimate partner.

By far, wives are the most frequent victims of fatal family violence. The *Bureau of Justice Statistics Special Report: National Crime Victimization Survey, Violence Against Women* reveals that 28 percent of annual brutality against women is perpetrated by a loved one compared to 5 percent against men.

In 1996, females were the victims of three of every four intimate murders and about 85 percent of nonlethal intimate violence.

(See *Friends and Relations*)

Swiss Cheese

Hard to stay neutral about Swiss cheese after hightailing it to the toilet. During the cheese's manufacture, an unwholesome bacteria can grow, giving eaters an uncivil case of scombroid poisoning, complete with burning mouths, a creeping rash, and a rampaging

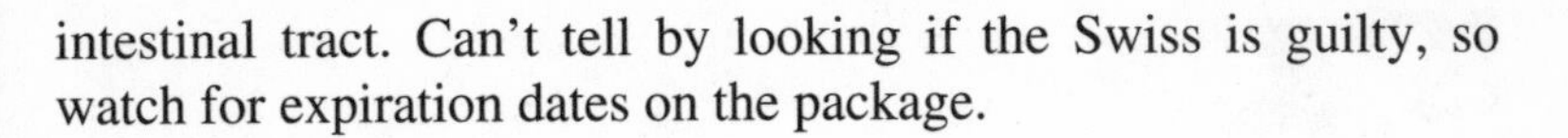

intestinal tract. Can't tell by looking if the Swiss is guilty, so watch for expiration dates on the package.

Taj Mahal

Unlicensed tour guides at the Taj Mahal, in cahoots with shady doctors and certain restaurants located near the Indian shrine, have devised a lucrative scam. The conniving escorts direct clueless tourists to eateries where they're served up tainted food. The tour guides then usher the hurling, food-poisoned sightseers to a conspiratorial doctor who collects a hefty fee for his medical services. The duplicitous team of schemers then divvy up the money.

You shouldn't visit the temple of love only to kneel at a porcelain throne. Follow a licensed tour leader.

Talcum Powder

Don't brush this off. Inhaling talcum powder can be more than a flaky health concern. Because the powder's tiny particles are easily carried into the lungs, pediatricians advise not to dust it on babies' bottoms. Instances of lung disease, severe pneumonia, and even deaths of infants have been attributed to talcum powder.

Women's groins are no-sprinkle zones, too, since researchers fear a possible link between ovarian cancer and talcum powder. The American Health Foundation reports that while the risk of acquiring ovarian cancer from using talcum powder is small, a more absorbent, safe-enough-to-eat alternative to consider is cornstarch powder.

Tallness

The *Harvard Public Health Review* reports that tallness is a risk factor for prostate, colon, and breast cancer. And, the NBA is concerned about the vagaries of player's unions?

(See *Shortness*)

Tanning Beds

I can't take a well-tanned person seriously.—Cleveland Amory

Millions of pasty-faced Americans (mostly young women) flock to tanning salons to bask in coffin-shaped beds glowing with Ultraviolet A light. The goal: to emerge Ipanema brown. Bulletin: The Bronze Age is over. Sautéing under UVA is anything but safe. It bears the very real perils of DNA damage, suppression of the immune system, retinal damage and cataracts, and a twofold increase for the calamitous skin cancer, melanoma.

Studies back up the notion that "healthy tan" is an oxymoron: Ultraviolet A radiation burns much deeper and more severely than Ultraviolet B rays, the sun's burning spectrum. Short-term skin maladies from a UVA fricassee include itching, redness, dryness, and rashes. More serious are the disfiguring skin cancers inflicted by UVA—basal cell and squamous cell carcinomas.

UVA damages the skin about forty times faster than the sun. Oh, what's a few wrinkles? No big deal, if you can't see them, which could happen since common UVA side effects are cataracts and retinal damage.

Dr. Heather Fork says because most of the harm from the ultraviolet light is time-delayed, it's difficult to convince the public of the adverse consequences of tanning beds. The Austin dermatologist suggests a smarter option for tan seekers: "Self-tanning creams and lotions create realistic tans for a fraction of the cost of a tanning salon membership, and are easy to use, and don't cause skin cancer. It's a win-win solution."

Don't be a fry baby. Stay out of the beds.

(See *Sunlight; Sunscreen*)

Tap Water

Forgot to take your medicine? Not to worry. Slug back a glass of tap water and you'll be good and dosed up.

Swedish and German scientists have discovered thirty common pharmaceuticals in municipal water supplies, including antibiotics, analgesics, antiseptics, cholesterol-lowering compounds, hormones, and chemotherapy and beta-blocker heart drugs. Officials at the U.S. Environmental Protection Agency weren't surprised by the findings, nor did they negate the possibility that the study could herald what might be congregating in America's water supply, if one were to look.

Tap water, regulated and considered perfectly safe by the EPA, is treated with chlorine (associated with a slightly elevated cancer risk in some studies and linked by others to an increased chance of miscarriage) that kills diseases like cholera and hepatitis; it's also doused with fluoride to guard against tooth decay. But the government's safety plan has a bug in it: The parasite *Cryptosporidium,* spread through fecal contamination and transmitted through municipal water systems, is highly resistant to chlorination. *Crytpo's* the germ that made Milwaukee infamous in 1993, when a major outbreak gave more than 400,000 people acute diarrhea and other intestinal problems. One hundred of the city's residents died during one of the nation's largest waterborne disease episodes.

The National Academy of Sciences grumbles that current EPA standards of allowable levels of arsenic in drinking water are set too low and fail to protect public health. The EPA agrees with the federal scientific panel's findings, although admits that a revised standard isn't likely to be in place until late 2000.

(See *Bottled Water*)

Teahouses

Trekkers' treat. The deaths of three hikers who passed away unexpectedly while sleeping in Nepalese teahouses over the past twelve years remain unexplained. Not accustomed to high tea perhaps.

Telephones

Dial *O* for *Oops*. Telephones ring the chimes of awkward callers, who sprain limbs tripping over cords, bonk teeth with receivers, and shatter foot bones with dropped instruments. About 14,400 of the telephone-challenged stumblebums took long-distance trips to emergency rooms in 1997.

Stay off the Princess during a thunderstorm. Lightning sparks every single thunderstorm, and the celestial fireworks can transmit heart-stopping electricity through phone lines.

Telescopes

It's an optical illusion to imagine that telescopes and binoculars are totally harmless. Hospital emergency rooms record stargazers' injuries, such as lacerated eyelids and scalps from shattered lenses, and shoulder sprains from lifting heavy instruments.

Televangelism

Don't touch that dial. People, especially those older than seventy-four, who worship the Gospel by remote control tend to have higher blood pressures than those who actually go—body and soul—to religious services.

After observing 4,000 older folks for six years (53 percent attended weekly services; 56 percent prayed daily; 75 percent tuned into religious TV or radio at least once a week), the Center for the Study of Religion/Spirituality at Duke University testifies that communicants who went to a church, synagogue, or other organized service at least once a week posted lower blood pressure readings than those who received the Scripture from TV or radio broadcasts.

(See *Religion*)

Television Sets

When there's nothing *on* television, make sure there's nobody *under* it. Newer models, large and light, are easily toppled, says the Radiological Society of North America, warning parents to keep an eye on children playing near a TV set.

Thanksgiving

You're as likely to break wind as bread during the orgy of consumption celebrated as Thanksgiving. The gut-stuffing holiday is the number one heartburn-inducing day of the year.

The ritual pilgrimage to the Thanksgiving table inevitably means getting the bird. Turkeys—more than 45 million are gobbled up on the family-gathering festive day—can carry salmonella and campylobacter bacteria. Avoid turkey à la puke; don't buy a prestuffed fowl (some experts say don't stuff the bird at all—keep the dressing in separate containers), cook it thoroughly, and store leftovers in the fridge.

(See *Leftovers*)

Therapy

Feeling angsty? Resolve it yourself. Couching it bluntly, psychologists have the highest suicide rate among the more than 230 occupations analyzed by epidemiologists at the National Institute for Occupational Safety and Health. The odds of a shrink doing the solo deed are 3.5 times greater than for those of the general public—and way ahead of dentists' ratio of 1.6, and even lawyers' 2.13 ratio.

Thin Thighs

People with thunder thighs may have a leg up on good health.

The skinnier the thighs, the greater the danger for having heart disease, claims a Stanford Medical School probe that evaluated health predictive factors, like the levels of cholesterol and triglycerides (fats in the blood) in moderately overweight men and women, and discovered that having hefty thighs seems to counteract the cardiac-disease risk of toting a portly pot.

In other fruitful studies, it's been proved that apple-shaped people who lug their fat around the gut run a higher susceptibility of heart disease than hipsters with pear-silhouettes.

Thunderstorms

It was a dark and stormy night. And doctors in England were deluged with a tenfold increase of patients wheezing with asthma, hay fever, and breathing problems. Physicians blamed the 1994 evening thunderstorms for the medical complaints, conjecturing that the heavy rainfall caused high concentrations of fungal spores and pollen.

Annually, 16 million thunderstorms pelt the earth, and each one produces lightning, the natural occurrence that kills more people than do tornadoes in any given year. Thunderstorms, not dinky downpours, are truly dangerous since they often lead to flash flooding (the numero uno thunderstorm killer with nearly 140 fatalities each year), hailstones falling at speeds faster than 100 mph, and strong winds and house-tossing tornadoes.

(See *Lightning; Mobile Homes*)

Tight Pants

Nothing comes between you and your denims. You wish. Buttocks, groin and thigh rashes are tight-pants-induced skin inflammations that doctors have tagged "jeans folliculitis."

Hang looser.

(See *Baggy Pants; Wearing Clothes*)

Toilets

Hate to dump this on you but it's best to be privy to bathroom dangers.

Americans don't seem well potty trained; the Consumer Product Safety Commission, giving a heads-up on the number of injuries in 1997, reports that an estimated 44,335 toilet-wounded were treated in emergency rooms for lacerations, broken bones, dislocated joints, and concussions. Most often, the injuries occur when people slip in the bathroom and land with a hard smack on the john's unforgiving porcelain. Some toilet sitters manage to miss the commode entirely, and wind up taking nasty tumbles. Fingers and penises are fractured (though not necessarily at the same time) by dropped toilet seats.

In loo of taking your business outside, caution seems to the watchword around toilets.

Tomato Sauce

Stored in moist containers, acidic tomato sauce can grow *Aspergillus flavus,* a mold that can make you very sick. With any luck, you'll barf it up quickly because the toxin can cause liver disease.

Don't try to salvage the sauce by scraping off the offending mold. Ditch it.

Toothbrushes

Potty training 101.

A single toilet flush contains thousands of disagreeable bacteria and viruses that are spewed from the bowl into the air. If your toothbrush is in target range, drops of *E. coli* bacteria will fall on the bristles, then you stick it in your mouth... get the drift?

To reap the rewards of a conscientiously applied program of dental hygiene, keep your toothbrush in the medicine cabinet.

(See *Medicine Cabinets; Toothpastes*)

Toothpastes

It's a flossed cause. Toothpaste tubes now bear a dire message warning overdosers to seek professional assistance or contact a Poison Control Center. Overdose? On toothpaste?

The caution on labels of all fluoride toothpastes, required by the FDA, is generating hundreds of calls from worried parents to manufacturers and poison control centers. The FDA responds that fluoride is a drug that's been associated with both acute and chronic toxicity, and any drug-product label must inform what to do in case of an overdose.

Brushing up on the subject, fluoride pastes are relatively safe. In 1997, not one of the 4,453 reported cases of unintended "fluoride exposure" was life-threatening. However, most toothpastes also contain sodium lauryl sulfate, a chemical that can make lips swell. But open wide—not your mouth, your eyes: An additive in many toothpastes is the disinfectant triclosan. Long regarded as the Big Daddy of bacteria killers, triclosan snuffs out all microbes. Sounds great, but the germ hunters at Tufts University Medical School worry that the indiscriminate use of triclosan—now found widely in soaps, kitchen sponges, fabrics, and plastic—could force the emergence of wonder bugs that the chemical will no longer be able to annihilate.

(See *Cleanliness*)

Trampolines

Boing boing. Bounce those playthings from the backyard. Trampoline injuries among children have tripled since 1990, to exceed 60,000 a year among kids eighteen and younger. Yet, sales of the springy platforms have increased fivefold, with 98 percent sold for home use. Calling for a ban on the sale of home trampolines, Dr. Gary A. Smith, director of the emergency department of Children's Hospital in Columbus, Ohio, spares few words in the medical journal *Pediatrics*: "I don't think trampolines have any place in homes or backyards. In no way should these things be considered toys."

Trampoliners suffer mostly cuts and bruises, sprains and fractures, and, although not as common, paralyzing spinal cord injuries and deaths (six at last count by the Consumer Product Safety Commission). Sometimes kids are hurt falling off trampolines, but more often they get banged up colliding with another jumping child, or by hitting an unpadded surface, such as a metal spring.

The effort to ban trampolines has had its ups and downs. Many schools have eliminated the activity from phys ed classes, and the American Academy of Pediatrics would like the bouncers removed from private homes as well. Recently accepted as an Olympic event, trampolining is likely to become a rage among kids if the competitive sport follows the popular course set in years past by figure skating and gymnastics. While dismissing the notion of a household ban, the Consumer Product Safety Commission agrees that trampolines should be made safer and carry stronger warning labels to help reduce the high injury rate.

Trying on Clothes

Those britches look lousy on you—truly lousy. *The New England Journal of Medicine* reports the tale of the clothing salesman who tried on trousers after his customers had put them on. Diagnosed with pubic lice, which is usually transmitted sexually, the gentleman claimed a year-long hanky-panky drought, so doctors presumed the slacker picked up the crab louse eggs from his trying habit.

Tug-of-War

The game of tug-of-war tests brute strength: all you need is a rope, two teams, and the winner yanks all. Simple and fun, as long as you don't get too wrapped up in it.

The Taiwanese organized a massive competition in Taipei with 1,600 contestants and one very long rope. Two tug-of-warriors wound the rope around their left arms for a better grip. Heave ho, heave ho. Uh oh. Both men's arms were ripped from their bodies. Croquet, anyone?

(See *Croquet*)

Tumbleweeds

Tumbleweeds that somersault across Richland, Washington, are radioactive. Sprouting on the large Hanford nuclear complex, a site that for years churned out plutonium for nuclear weapons, water-seeking tumbleweeds, with roots that stretch 15 feet into the radioactive soil, suck up heavily contaminated groundwater. All's fine until the top of the plant, blown off by heavy breezes, rolls away, shimmering radioactivity in its wake.

Will the Department of Energy's multibillion-dollar site cleanup rein in the radioactive tumblers, as well as exterminate the area's hot ants, flies, and gnats? The answer is glowin' in the wind, pal.

Two-Lane Roads

You're noodling along back roads and blue highways, with freeway road ragers and spaghetti belts in the rearview mirror. Seems an ideal excursion, but get out the map. About three-fourths of all traffic fatalities occur on two-lane roads.

Curvy blacktops, with narrow lanes, steep slopes, and railroad crossings have the highest crash rates, and few, if any, safety features, such as breakaway road signs or rumble strips that sound a warning if a car drives off the road. Many of the two-lane accidents involve crashing into trees and hitting utility poles and bridge supports, obstacles not often located on superhighways.

Underpants Before Socks

In brief: Putting on skivvies before donning a pair of socks could spread athlete's foot to your groin, causing a prickly dose of jock itch. To keep athlete's foot from hitchhiking northward, the Ohio Dermatological Association recommends, après shower, towel down, not up, your body.

Underwire Bras

Lightning blanches a darkened sky. Quick—what's the first thing to do? Shed your bra. Advice too late for the twenty-three-year-old struck by lightning while strolling through an Austrian park; she was killed when the skybolt zinged straight for her metal underwire brassiere. In September 1999, two women fizzled out in Hyde Park, their deaths attributed to lightning-conducting bras. That's some lift and separate.

Luckier was the young woman who lived after being struck by lightning at the June 1998 Tibetan Freedom Concert at RFK Memorial Stadium in Washington, D.C. Talking on a cell phone, she was zapped through her right ear by more than 1 million watts of nature's electricity. Her metal-supported brassiere conducted the bolt through her body, causing cardiac arrest and third-degree chest, face, and thigh burns. If she'd not been wearing that bra, trauma surgeons presumed that her injuries might have been less severe. Breast assured, one can only hope the resilient woman now wears a padded undergarment.

(See *Telephones; Wearing Clothes*)

Uneven Fingers

A man's shoe size may or may not match his, um, IQ, but research at England's University of Liverpool asserts there's a definite link between finger length and fertility.

Measuring the hands of men and women at an infertility clinic, the investigators determined that the men with the least symmetrical hands (hands that weren't mirror images of each other) had the lowest sperm counts, and what sperm the men had were less active. Both conditions make infertility more likely. In *New Scientist*, research author and evolutionary biologist, Dr. John Manning says, "Digit asymmetry predicts the number of sperm per ejaculate. The more asymmetry, the fewer sperm."

Men's ring fingers are usually longer than their index fingers; women's tend to be the same length. Dr. Manning's inquiry points out that men with ring fingers much longer than their index fingers have higher levels of testosterone, the male sex hormone that plays a role in fertility. The opposite holds for women: a longer index finger is associated with higher levels of estrogen, the female hormone essential for reproduction.

Dr. Manning, while encouraged by the evidence linking finger size and sex traits, cautions that people shouldn't count on hand signals to determine if they will procreate. Further studies are underway to confirm the finger/fertility link.

Urinals

For some guys, the number one affliction is shy bladder syndrome—the bashful inability to use the rest room if someone is close enough to see or hear. Afflicting some 17 million Americans (mostly men, although some women are bathroom squeamish, too), the performance anxiety is more than an inconvenience: Unreleased urine can back up into the ureters to cause kidney problems. The tinkle timid should make a pit stop at a urologist.

V

Vacuum Cleaners

Piles of statistics tell the story: every year, thousands of people with vacuum cleaner–inflicted injuries are swept to hospital emergency rooms with wrenched backs and smashed fingers, lacerated cheeks, and corneal abrasions, which usually happen after tripping over the electrical cords or the sweeper itself, or from a sharp blow from the metal nozzle.

Although it helps, you don't have to be maladroit to get hosed. The typical household vacuum cleaner, according to the EPA, emits millions of fine, easily inhaled particles that can become embedded deep in the lungs and aggravate asthma, cause bronchitis, and generate severe allergy symptoms.

Vegetarianism

Makes you want to blow beets. Going meatless could be a signal of bulimia and anorexia in young athletic women, admonishes *The Physician and Sports Medicine.* The medical journal makes mention of several studies that link veggie diets with eating disorders, including an investigation that found that girls who didn't eat meat dieted twice as often, vomited four times as often, and used laxatives eight times as often as meat eaters. Meat-shunning female jocks also run the risk of developing protein, iron, and zinc deficiencies.

Vending Machines

Late for a hot date? No sweat. Get whatever you need in a hurry—flowers, breath mints, condoms, live bait—with a little pocket change and the push of a button. Vending machines are convenient purveyors of millions of products, but don't try to get a freebie by rocking one back and forth. The machines can weigh as much as 1,000 pounds, and with high centers of gravity, topple over easily. The injuries can be gruesome, reports *The Journal of the American Medical Association*—skull and pelvis fractures, punctured bladders, and bleeding brains. The Consumer Product Safety Commission reports at least 37 deaths and 113 injuries between 1978 and 1995 from falling vending machines.

Vigilance

Put this book down. Casting an eye out for dangers could scare up heart problems.

University of Pittsburgh psychologists, defining vigilance as "a chronic search for potential threats from other people or things in the environment," studied a group of men in various threatening circumstances, and concluded that even a mild state of wariness increases blood pressure and heart rate readings, which, in the long run, could compromise good health and hurt book sales.

Visual Aids

The New England Journal of Medicine published the sticky plight of the man who, in preparation for a scientific presentation, raised a gruesome blister on his thumb by jamming eighty pushpins through thick poster board. Later, the blister ruptured when he dismantled the visual aid. The maimed presenter recalled (as did other show-and-tellers) suffering the agony of past blister injuries from pressing thumbtacks into ungiving materials. Tagging the condition "poster presenter's thumb," a physician suggests that organizations provide user-friendly poster board to help prevent similar tragic incidents.

Volleyball

Side out. Volleyball doesn't seem to be a brutalizing sport, but it nets its share of injuries. Feet and ankles take the brunt of the hurt, with most sprains occurring at the net during a blocking move. Inflamation of the delicate Achilles tendons and of knees are common complaints, as are shoulder, wrist, hand, and finger injuries.

W

Walking

Here's something to think about on your evening walk: You're 1.6 times more likely to get killed by a car while out for a stroll than you are to be shot and killed by a stranger.

More than 6,000 pedestrians are struck and killed by vehicles each year, and more than 110,000 are injured. Most of the cities on the survey's top ten worst places to walk are in the urban-sprawled South and West. The five having a foothold as the most perilous metro areas for walkers: Fort Lauderdale; Miami; Atlanta; Tampa–St. Petersburg–Clearwater; and Dallas. Among the safest: New York City; Boston; Pittsburgh; and Milwaukee.

Most vulnerable are senior citizen peds, who need to take steps to keep from getting whacked while crossing the street. Fewer than 1 percent of people over seventy-two years old are able to walk fast enough—2.7 miles per hour—to make it across an average intersection before the light changes, says the *American Journal of Public Health*.

Mean as the city streets are, a barefoot stroll in the grass could nail you, too. Sharp pointy things lay in wait, eager to jab deep into your sole. Tetanus shots hurt; wear shoes.

(See *Florida; Shoes*)

Washing Dishes

You're soaking in it. *It* could be a bloody mess if you immerse your hands in soapy water and grab a knife or broken glass.

(See *Dishwashers*)

Watches

Time and again, emergency rooms tend to people with facial cuts and hand lacerations from sharp-edged watches. Doctors also mend tykes who've swallowed batteries and adults with shock burns from touching their wristwatch to electrical equipment.

Watching Television

Television is an invention that permits you to be entertained in your living room by people you wouldn't have in your home.—David Frost

A sixth-grader has been a witness to thousands of murders, and she's expected to play nice with her little brother?

The American Psychological Association asserts that kids—starting as young as two years old—spend an average of 35 to 55 hours every week in the vast wasteland of television shows, videos, and video games. Claiming that 61 percent of TV programming contains violence, the National Television Violence Study broadcasts that each year children have a front row seat to an estimated 10,000 murders, beatings, stabbings, rapes, and shootings.

TV-watching kids may or may not be getting psychologically screwed up watching reruns of *My Mother the Car,* but at least there's no physical harm done. Maybe. Maybe not. Youngsters who spend most of their free time watching the tube are at greater risk of injury than kids who engage in potentially dangerous sports and activities, say medical scientists who interviewed 221 children injured in accidents and taken to emergency rooms with fractures, burns and multiple contusions. Most of the banged-up tykes were habitual TV viewers. *Archives of Pediatrics and Adolescent Medicine* editor Dr. Catherine DeAngelia discerns a definite parallel and poses that certain risky conduct is stimulated by watching violence on TV: "Only control over the number of hours that children spend watching television will have any influence on the rate of juvenile injuries."

Water Balloons

Launched by slingshots, water balloons can put a big damper on fun.

Forceful as some rifle bullets, the rubbery projectiles can perforate corneas, hemorrhage retinas, lacerate eyelids, and fracture eye sockets. Ophthalmologists warn that any "toy" that can explode a watermelon from 20 feet away must be regarded as a serious threat to vision.

Water Beds

Therapeutic to some, erotic to others, water beds are a gurgling menace. Ask the wave of people—some 4,000—treated during 1997 in emergency rooms for cuts and bruises, fractures, and sprains from falling off of, running into, or trying to move the quivering pods of liquid.

Water Parks

Come on in, the water's fine. Well, not really. Public pools are swimming with raunchy bacteria that can infect eyes, ears, and intestinal tracts. Maybe you enjoy paddling around with hundreds of sun-stroked strangers, but before taking the plunge, remember that kiddos often regard the pool as potty. Fecal microorganisms cause cholera, typhoid fever, and dysentery. In 1998, after playing in an Atlanta water park's wading pool, eight children were stricken with a truculent form of *E. coli* bacterium traced to a defecating-in-the-water child.

The lifeguarding Department of Agriculture issued an alert the summer of 1999 about another infectious parasite that could be backstroking in many swimming pools and water parks since current chlorine levels aren't strong enough to kill the critter. *Cryptosporidium parvum,* primarily a waterborne disease, is transmitted by human feces. It's fairly easy to become infected with *Crypto*; all it takes is accidentally swallowing a small amount of contaminated water. Symptoms—diarrhea, stomach cramps, and fever—can last two weeks. As yet, no drug exists that will knock the noxious bacteria from the body.

Drownings occur most often in residential swimming pools, but the number of injuries linked to water parks, with undulating wave pools and 250-foot plunges, more than doubled from 1994 to 1997. Towering water slides with twisting chutes make a big splash, leaving some wave riders with bloody noses, sore backs, and loose teeth. Medical journals report horrifying stories of vaginal and cervical evisceration of female water-chute sliders.

The Consumer Product Safety Commission describes incidents of hair, arms, and legs getting entangled on pool drains (some resulting in drownings) and of the disembowelment of children sitting on drains in public wading pools.

(See *Lifeguarding*)

Watering the Lawn

Triptoe through the tulips. Garden hoses disperse an estimated 12,577 people to hospitals every year, spouts the Consumer Product Safety Commission.

Pray for rain.

(See *Yard Work*)

Give wide berth to anybody named Wayne.

Bad boys reside in Waynes' world: John Wayne Gacy, the clown-painting serial killer; Wayne Williams, Atlanta's child murderer; Larry Wayne Harris, the convicted bubonic plague–buying, biological terrorist; Wayne Boden, Canada's "Vampire Rapist"; and Georgia-executed murderer, Ellis Wayne Felker.

The Kabalarian Philosophy—a Vancouver, B.C., group with an odd name itself—analyzes how a person's name relates to personality, and posts the analysis on its website: "Intelligence, as a universal power, is expressed consciously only through language, and your name gives you your individual intelligent expression." Okay. According to the Kabalarians, the appellation Wayne "creates very caustic moods which prevent harmony in close associations."

The name calling never wanes: Oregon murderer and lifer Richard Wayne Godwin; Wayne, the hateful brother on *The Wonder Years*; Conan Wayne Hale, sentenced to death for the 1995 murders of three teens; early-released-from-prison Robert Wayne Shelton, rapist and murderer; Wayne Pierce, former Klan leader who served time on a weapons charge; John Wayne Glover, the Australian "Granny Killer"; and lifer, Earl Wayne Henley, Texas serial killer.

Weak Hands

Limp means gimp.

The weaker your middle-aged grasp, the more likely you'll be a disabled geezer. Measuring the hand-grip strength of about 6,000 men in 1965, and then again twenty-five years later, the Honolulu Heart Program discovered that the men who had an anemic 1960s handshake were, a quarter of a century later, two times more likely to be functionally limited than the strong grippers—they walked slower than normal, had to use their arms to get up from a chair, and suffered more illnesses and infirmities.

Attributing low muscle strength as a cause of physical disability, researchers assert that grip strength is a good indication of overall strength, and recommend strengthening exercises for men and women of all ages.

(See *Strong Hands*)

Wearing Clothes

How difficult is it to get dressed? For some people, the answer must be "very."

In 1997, some 50,000 clothes-calls seen by emergency room doctors included a middle-aged man who fractured his knee pulling on a pair of pants, and another fellow who dislocated a shoulder when taking off his shirt. A thirty-eight-year-old woman, bending over to slip on her undies, strained her lower back; one teenager twisted her knee yanking on jeans, while another tripped on her trousers and lurched down a flight of stairs. Some of the sartorially wounded, standing too close to open stoves, suffered severe burns when their loose-fitting clothes were set ablaze.

(See *Baggy Pants; Brassieres; Shoes; Socks; Tight Pants; Underwire Bras; Zippers*)

Weekends

No, it's not your imagination. Weekends are rainier—at least in urban areas—than the rest of the week, during which airborne pollutants build up and trap heat in the upper air, causing more clouds and showers to dampen your outdoor plans. Rain-slick streets make driving on mean weekend streets even more dangerous.

(See *Fridays; Saturdays*)

Well-Done

You choose: the big E or the big C.

E. coli frolics in undercooked meat; the best way to hammer the ruthless bacteria is to cook meat to a philistine doneness, which disregards a National Cancer Institute's study that reveals a link between well-done meat and stomach cancer, and which also neglects to consider findings of an Iowa research project claiming that eating charred meat hikes the risk of breast cancer more than 4.5 times higher than eating rare or medium-cooked meats.

Wheelchairs

Half of the 1.5 million Americans in wheelchairs suffer from carpal tunnel syndrome. Repetitive stress injuries, caused by gripping and pushing the wheel rims, pinch nerves and damage tendons in wheelchair users' shoulders, arms, and hands. A National Institutes of Health study is analyzing movement techniques in order to determine the least injurious positions for wheelchair users and to find ways to help doctors and therapists provide better training.

White Coats

It's not a before Labor Day fashion thing but rather a mysterious malady that makes some people freak in a medical setting. The vision of a white coat sends their usually normal blood pressure to skyrocket levels. Researchers declare that more than a third of patients with mild to moderately high blood pressure may suffer from white-coat hypertension and could be vulnerable to heart disease and stroke.

Winter

Winter can truly be the unbearable darkness of being. As days shorten, some 10 million Americans, sufferers of seasonal affective disorder, become depressed and lethargic. The down-in-the-dumpers lose sexual interest, binge on carbos and sweets, tend to sleep a lot, and feel irritable, fatigued, and blue. Doctors warn of SAD's possible serious health implications and recommend basking as long as 30 minutes each morning under high-intensity artificial illumination that mimics beneficial sunlight.

If you prefer to banish the doldrums a more natural way, head outdoors for a stroll during the brightest part of the day. The natural sunlight helps readjust the body's daily rhythms, but mild as it is, winter's sun can damage your skin. Be diligent about applying sunscreen. Unfortunately, most Americans—98 percent—don't bother with the protection during winter months, reports the American Academy of Dermatology. Not smart. UVA rays, which age the skin by penetrating deep into dermal layers and play a role in causing skin cancer, don't vary in strength by season or time of day.

The nationwide incidence of heart attacks—in men and women—is 53 percent higher in the winter months than during the summer. The tremendous exertion of snow shoveling has taken the rap for this seasonal surge but, according to recent studies, it's Sunbelters who have the largest increase (75 percent) in the number of winter cardiac failures. Inactivity seems to be the biggest bugaboo: Americans are slugs during the winter, no matter where they live, and scientists correlate this seasonal couch-slouching peak with the rise in heart attacks.

(See *Autumn; Cold Weather; January; Spring; Summer; Sunlight*)

Women in Labor

In a small study (inspired by childbirth educators who tried to persuade researchers that women don't really scream during labor; all that yowling is to "joyfully welcome" the event), the decibel levels of thirty childbirthing women were measured. None of the moms-to-be were given pain medication (at their request) and all reported suffering severe labor pains.

"The scream that some of these patients make is ear piercing," recounts obstetrician Dr. David J. Birnbach of St. Luke's–Roosevelt Hospital Center in New York City. The loudest mother registered

115 decibels from 1 yard away, about the distance a monitor-tending nurse would stand. Here's a sound check: From 5 feet away, an ambulance siren measures 120 decibels; a screeching subway, 100 decibels.

The Occupational Safety and Health Administration requires workers who are exposed to sounds louder than 90 decibels for 8 continuous hours, or 102 decibels for 4 hours, to wear ear protection. Dr. Birnbach figures that anyone (nurses as well as friends and family) standing close to a yelping whelper who registers 100 decibels for every three-minutes-apart-contraction could be exposed to sound levels that exceed the OSHA safety limits.

Following delivery, the mothers were asked if they would opt to give birth again this time without using pain medication; 65 percent said of course they would. Probably couldn't hear the question.

(See *Earplugs*)

Woodstoves

Cooking and heating with woodstoves may increase the incidence of cancers of the mouth and throat. People regularly exposed to the potbellied smoke have two to three times the risk of these cancers, draws out a Brazilian medical study.

Woodworking

Woodworking is plane dangerous. Home workshop equipment mutilates thousands of would-be carpenters every year. Even the raw materials—dead trees—can cause knotty problems. If the skin allergies, inflamed eyes, and lung problems that are linked to hardwoods and toxic glues aren't enough to whittle your woody for the pastime, perhaps the liver-damaging pesticides and preservatives found in many of the woods will shelve all interest.

Everybody needs a hobby, but preferably one that won't damage several senses. Noisy woodworking machines cranked up as high as 110 decibels can cause hearing loss; over time, vibrating tools will numb fingers and hands, leading to permanent nerve damage; wood chips and splinters are not easy on the eyes. Wood shops can easily go up in smoke since electrical equipment and fine sawdust make for explosive fire hazards.

Shop around for something safer to do.

(See *Do-It-Yourselfing*)

Yard Sales

Haggle smart. Unsafe items are unloaded at yard and garage sales all the time, especially products for kids that manufacturers or the Consumer Product Safety Commission have recalled for safety reasons. Like bunk beds that can strangle tots, bean bag chairs (12 million have been recalled after thirty pellet-choking incidences), child-suffocating old cribs, collapsing playpens, and rickety baby carriages.

(See *Bean Bag Chairs; Halogen Floor Lamps; Recliner Chairs*)

Yard Work

What price morning glories! Compost cooties, killer bees, nasty birds, wicked tools. Toiling the soil is thorny business.

Dirt is dirty. Hiding in soil and compost heaps is a rascally organism, *Clostribium tetani,* which causes tetanus (also called lockjaw because first, victims have trouble swallowing, and later, difficulty breathing) if it creeps into an open wound—which could come from the hornets, wasps, or bees like those that fatally stung fifty-nine people in 1995. Garden tools wreak bodily harm;

the National Safety Council reports that more than 68,200 gardeners petaled to hospital emergency rooms in 1996.

Birds doo it. A 1998 study published in *The Lancet* reports most of the sixteen people who fell ill in an Australian outbreak of psittacosis, a potentially fatal disease spread by inhaling the dust from bird droppings, were infected while working in their yards.

Injuries, stings, and cuts aside, you enjoy puttering around the garden. Sputtering is more like it if you're into heavy-duty pesticiding. Throwing caution and toxins to the wind, Americans spend a whopping $30 billion a year scattering 70 million pounds of weed-killing poisons to lush up their yards. Most of the pesticide on the market today is more than ten times as toxic as chemicals used back in the fifties so watch where you're spraying the stuff; vegetable gardens, swimming pools, and neighborhood water supplies seem to have an aversion to poison.

Cover up: Your hands are most likely to be exposed, although your forehead, abdomen, and (yikes!) crotch absorb pesticides faster than other body parts. Wear a hat, gloves, long sleeves, and goggles.

Gardening tip of the day: Buy a condo.

(See *Brightly Colored Clothes; Cut Grass; Dark-Colored Clothes; Leaf Blowers; Mowing the Lawn; Sunlight*)

Yoga

Some positions aren't worth taking. The popularity of the mind-body exercise of yoga has spawned a bevy of teachers with limited yoga or fitness training, and the not-so-supple joints of adherents—especially aging boomers—are responding unkindly. "Sometimes it seems that the only thing growing more quickly than the number of yoga classes offered in fitness facilities is the number of injuries sustained by eager participants," says Mara Carrico in *IDEA Health & Fitness Source* magazine, describing a new "health and fitness" aerobized yoga, which can be vigorous and physically demanding. Carrico warns that some beginning yoga students aren't capable of the body-braiding exercises and that untrained instructors may not spot potential problems.

Yo-Yos

Dentists are reeling about the tooth-cracking dangers of yo-yos. Even the *British Medical Journal* is spinning: "A yo-yo in unskilled and overenthusiastic hands becomes a lethal projectile that can smash treasured family objects and remove children's teeth with ease."

Yo-yos can whirl as fast as 11,000 rpm. "Shoot the moon," "skin the cat," and "around the world" are considered highly dangerous, the maneuvers most likely to flail the hard plastic yo-yo back into the face to shatter molars.

Parents, mind dentists' warning: For very young, uncoordinated children: No yo-yo, ma.

Zippers

Poor skin.

Circumcise annual emergency room reports. Among the clothing-related injuries you'll find dozens of penile abrasions and lacerations. Tuck, then cover.

(See *Wearing Clothes*)

REFERENCES

Abstinence	*British Medical Journal*
Acne Medicine	U.S. Food and Drug Administration
Aerosol Containers	E.R. Watch; U.S. Consumer Product Safety Commission
Afternoons	University of Washington, Seattle
Airplane Aisle Seats	Association of Flight Attendants; *New York Times*
Alaska	*Accident Facts*, National Safety Council
Alfalfa Sprouts	*Journal of the American Medical Association*
Alligator Shoes	*Europa Times*
Aluminum Foil	E.R. Watch; U.S. Consumer Product Safety Commission
Antennas	U.S. Consumer Product Safety Commission
Apple Juice	U.S. Food and Drug Administration
Apricot Kernels	*Annals of Emergency Medicine*
Aromatherapy	American Council on Science and Health; *Health Foods Business*
Artificial Nails	*Archives of Pediatric and Adolescent Medicine*
Assertivenesss	*Psychology Today*
Astringents	National Rosacea Society
August	*Accident Facts*, National Safety Council
Autumn	*Asthma and Allergy Foundation of America*
Baby-Faced Boys	*Journal of Personality and Social Psychology*
Backpacks	U.S. Consumer Product Safety Commission; American Academy of Pediatrics Committee on School Health
Bad Initials	University of California
Bagels	*Washington Post*
Baggy Pants	U.S. Consumer Product Safety Commission
Baked Potatoes	*Journal of Infectious Diseases*

Bakeries	*Cincinnati Enquirer*
Baking Soda	*Medical Data Exchange*
Balloons	*British Medical Journal*
Banisters	U.S. Consumer Product Safety Commission
Bartending	U.S. Bureau of Labor; University of California at San Francisco
Bathing Suits	*British Medical Journal*
Batteries	U.S. Consumer Product Safety Commission
Beaches	Natural Resource Defense Council; U.S. Consumer Product Safety Commission
Bean Bag Chairs	U.S. Consumer Product Safety Commission
Beauty Parlors	*The Lancet*
Between 3 P.M. and 4 P.M.	Fight Crime: Invest in Kids
Bible Quoting	Associated Press
Bicycle Seats	Boston University School of Medicine
Bicycle Wheels	U.S. Consumer Product Safety Commission
Birmingham, Alabama	*American Demographics*
Blow Dryers	U.S. Consumer Product Safety Commission
Blowing Off Steam	*Journal of Personality and Social Psychology*
Blowing Your Nose	*Millbrook News*
Blue Eyes	*Ophthalmology*
Body Odor	*The Lancet*
Bottled Water	Natural Resources Defense Council
Bottling Up Anger	*Journal of Epidemiology and Community Health*; Reuters Health
Bowing	*Daily Record*
Bowl Games	*New England Journal of Medicine*
Braids	U.S. Food and Drug Administration; *Family Practice News*
Brassieres	*Nutrition Health Review; Dressed to Kill: The Link Between Breast Cancer and Bras*
Bread	Johns Hopkins Inteli-Health, Inc.
Brie	U.S. Centers for Disease Control and Prevention
Brightly Colored Clothes	Ivanhoe Broadcast News, Inc.
Brush Cutters	U.S. Consumer Product Safety Commission
Bubble Baths	Healthcentral.Com
Bug Zappers	Entomological Society of America
Camping	University of California at San Diego; National Parks and Conservation Association; National Parks Service
Candles	National Fire Protection Association

Canned Tuna	U.S. Food and Drug Administration
Can Openers	U.S. Consumer Product Safety Commission
Cardboard Boxes	*New York Times*
Careers in Advertising	U.S. Bureau of Labor Statistics
Car Phones	University of Toronto; Insurance Institute for Highway Safety
Car-Pool Lanes	*Wall Street Journal*
Car Windows	Skin Cancer Foundation
Cartoons	*Journal of the American Medical Association*
Casinos	Thirdage Media
Casseroles	*Washington Post*
Cats	*Pediatrics*
Cereal	U.S. Centers for Disease Control and Prevention
Chain Saws	The Mining Company; *Occupational Health & Safety*
Chamomile Tea	National Food Safety Database
Champagne	American Academy of Ophthalmology
Cheerleading	National Cheerleading Association
Chewing Gum	*Pediatrics*
Chilies	American Family Physician
Chopsticks	*The Lancet*
Christmas	National Fire Protection Association; Associated Press; Reuters
Chubby Cheeks	*New England Journal of Medicine*
Cigars	Boston University School of Dental Medicine
Cinnamon Gum	University of Louisville
City Biking	National Highway Traffic Safety Administration
Classical Performances	*Academic Emergency Medicine*
Cleanliness	U.S. Centers for Disease Control and Prevention; Tufts University School of Medicine
Close Shaves	U.S. Food and Drug Administration
Clothespins	U.S. Consumer Product Safety Commission
Coffee Cups	University of Arizona
Cold Weather	Lille University School of Medicine
Contact Lenses	American Academy of Ophthalmology
Cook-in-the-Bag Foods	Agricultural Research Service
Cookbooks	*New York Times*
Cookie Dough	U.S. Food and Drug Administration
Cookie Sheets	U.S. Food and Drug Administration

Cookware U.S. Consumer Product Safety Commission
Coping *Psychology Today*
Cosmetic Counters U.S. Food and Drug Administration
Coworkers U.S. Bureau of Labor Statistics
Cracking Knuckles *Scientific American*
Crayons U.S. Consumer Product Safety Commission
Croquet *British Medical Journal*
Crossing Your Legs Vein Treatment Center
Crying *Headache*
Crystal Ware Medical Data Exchange
Curling Irons U.S. Consumer Product Safety Commission
Cut Grass *Geophysical Research Letters*
Cutting Boards University of Arizona

Dallas–Fort Worth State Farm Mutual Automobile Insurance Company; Surface Transportation Policy Project
Dark-Colored Clothes *Annals of Internal Medicine*
Daylight Savings Time *New England Journal of Medicine*
Daytime U.S. Bureau of Justice
Deer Insurance Information Institute
Deli Meats U.S. Centers for Disease Control and Prevention
Deodorant British Broadcasting Company
Dieting *Science*; *Circulation*; Rutgers University; University of Pittsburgh
Dinner Music *Scandinavian Journal of Caring Sciences*
Dirty Mouths University of Minnesota
Dishwashers U.S. Consumer Product Safety Commission
Do-It-Yourselfing U.S. Consumer Product Safety Commission
Doctors' Writing *British Medical Journal*
Dogs Humane Society of the United States
Dolphins *New York Times*
Dominating Conversations *Journal of the American Psychosomatic Society*
Doorbells *Journal of the American College of Cardiology*
Doors U.S. Consumer Product Safety Commission
Douching University of Pittsburgh
Downsizing *The Lancet*
Drinking Fountains U.S. Consumer Product Safety Commission
Driving at Night National Safety Council
Driving in New Hampshire National Transportation Safety Board
Driving Music University of Sydney

Drowsy Truckers Stanford University Sleep Research Center; National Highway Traffic Safety Administration

Drumsticks *New York Times*

Dry-cleaned Clothes U.S. Department of Health and Human Services

Ear Candling U.S. Food and Drug Administration

Earlobe Creases *American Journal of Medicine*; *American Journal of Cardiology*

Earplugs U.S. Consumer Product Safety Commission

Eating Out *American Journal of Public Health*

Educations *Journal of the American Medical Association*

Egg Cartons *Consumer Research Magazine*

Eggnog U.S. Food and Drug Administration

Eggs U.S. Agriculture Department; Center for Science in the Public Interest

Electrolysis U.S. Food and Drug Administration

Elevators Elevator Escalator Safety Foundation; *Boston Globe*

Empty Day Books *Journal of the American Medical Association*; *Newsweek*; Survey Research Center, University of Michigan; Stanford University

Escalators U.S. Consumer Product Safety Commission

Expensive Athletic Shoes *British Journal of Sports Medicine*

Eyeglasses U.S. Consumer Product Safety Commission

Fallen Leaves Loyola University Medical Center Injury Prevention Program

Fashion Magazines Harvard Medical School; Harvard School of Public Health

Fat Necks *Thorax*

Faucets U.S. Consumer Product Safety Commission

Fire Engines *Auto and Road User Journal*

Firing Someone *Circulation*

First Week of the Month *New England Journal of Medicine*

Fish Tanks *Journal of Accident and Emergency Medicine*

Fishing *Infections in Medicine; Field and Stream*

Five Servings a Day U.S. Centers for Disease Control and Prevention

Fizzy Drinks *New England Journal of Medicine*

Flaming Drinks *American Surgeon*

Florida	Surface Transportation Policy Project; Environmental Working Group; Florida Game and Fresh Water Fish Commission; University of Florida
Flower Shows	Associated Press
Football Games	ABC News
French Fries	National Cancer Institute; *Consumer Reports on Health*
Frequent Flying	Air Transport Association; Federal Aviation Agency; *New York Times*; Association of Flight Attendants; *New Scientist*
Fridays	*Accident Facts*, National Safety Council
Friends and Relations	Bureau of Justice
Frosted Eye Shadow	American Academy of Ophthalmology
Frozen Beef Patties	*British Medical Journal*
Furnaces	U.S. Consumer Product Safety Commission
Gemstones	*British Broadcasting Company*
George Costanza	*Catheterization and Cardiovascular Diagnosis*
Ginseng Extract	Federal Bureau of Alcohol, Tobacco and Firearms
Glasgow	Dundee University
Glue Guns	U.S. Consumer Product Safety Commission
Goalposts	U.S. Consumer Product Safety Commission
Goggles	*Postgraduate Medical Journal*
Golf	American Academy of Dermatology; U.S. Consumer Product Safety Commission; *British Medical Journal*; *Gut*; American Orthopaedic Society for Sports Medicine
Gospel Concerts	*Academic Emergency Medicine*
Grapefruit Juice	U.S. Food and Drug Administration
Gray Beards	*New England Journal of Medicine*
Guacamole	U.S. Food and Drug Administration
Guardrails	University of Cincinnati
Hairbrushes	U.S. Consumer Product Safety Commission
Hair Conditioners	*Allergy*
Hair Gel	British Broadcasting Company
Halloween	U.S. Department of Health and Human Services
Halogen Floor Lamps	U.S. Consumer Product Safety Commission
Handlebars	*Pediatrics*
Hangovers	Kuopio Ischemic Heart Disease Risk Factor Study

Hedgehogs	*Archives of Dermatology*
Heimlich Maneuver	Stanford University Medical Center
Herbal Cigarettes	U.S. Centers for Disease Control and Prevention
Herbal Skin Creams	*British Medical Journal*
High-Definition TV	*American Academy of Family Physicians*
Home Canning	U.S. Food and Drug Administration
Home Fitness Equipment	U.S. Consumer Product Safety Commission
Horseback Riding	*Journal of Family Practice*
Hospitals	*New England Journal of Medicine; The Lancet*
Hot Baths	U.S. Consumer Product Safety Commission
Hot Dogs	University of Southern California School of Medicine; *Wall Street Journal*
Hot Food	*New England Journal of Medicine*
Hot Showers	Columbia University Health Education Program
Hot Tubs	U.S. Centers for Disease Control and Prevention; *Washington Post*; National Institutes of Health
Hotel Rooms	Johns Hopkins School of Public Health
Hugging Daddy	*Pediatrics*
Humidifiers	*Health*
Ice Cream	Temple University Health Science Center
Ice Cubes	Mayo Clinic
Impotence	Loyola University Medical Center
Internet	Carnegie Mellon University
Intersections	Insurance Institute for Highway Safety
January	University of Massachusetts Medical School; *Journal of the American College of Cardiology*
January Birthdays	American Psychological Society
Jerky	*British Medical Journal*
Jewelry	American Academy of Dermatology; American Dental Association
Jimsonweed	New Jersey Poison Control Center
Juice Bars	CBS Worldwide, Inc.
July	National Center for Health Statistics; National Safety Council; American Dietetic Association; U.S. Consumer Product Safety Commission
Kentucky	U.S. Centers for Disease Control and Prevention; *American Demographics*

Keys	U.S. Consumer Product Safety Commission
Kissing a Dog	American Veterinary Medical Association
Kneeling	*Mayo Clinic Health Letter*
Lakes	U.S. Centers for Disease Control and Prevention
Landing a Punch	St. Luke's–Roosevelt Hospital
Laundry	University of Arizona
Leaf Blowers	*Washington Post*
Leaky Pipes	*New York Times; Caduceus*
Leather Jackets	*Fresno Bee*
Leftovers	*Tufts University Health & Nutrition Letter; New York Times*
Leis	*British Medical Journal*
Licorice	*University of California at Berkeley Wellness Letter; New England Journal of Medicine*
Lifeguarding	*Occupational and Environmental Medicine; The Lancet*
Lightning	Lightning Data Center; Heart Information Network
Liposuction	American Society of Plastic and Reconstructive Surgeons
Lipstick	*Daily Record*
Liver Spots	drweil.com
Lizards	*Pediatrics*
Long Faces	Academy of General Dentistry
Long Hours	*British Medical Journal; Occupational and Environmental Medicine*
Long Underwear	*Men's Health*
Loofahs	*Journal of Clinical Microbiology*
Love Connections	*Journal of the American Medical Association*
Love Handles	*The Lancet; Journal of the American Medical Association*
Low Cholesterol	*Psychosomatic Medicine*
Luggage	U.S. Consumer Product Safety Commission
Luggage Carts	*American Journal of Ophthalmology*
Maine's Route 201	State of Maine; *New York Times*
Making Music	*Neurology*
Male Pattern Baldness	Physicians Health Study
Malls	*USA Today; Good Housekeeping*
Mangoes	*New England Journal of Medicine*

Maraschino Cherries	*Cocktail*
Marital Spats	University of Utah
Marshmallows	*American Family Physician*
Martinis	*New England Journal of Medicine*
Mascara	U.S. Food and Drug Administration
Mattresses	*Allergy*
Medical Consent Forms	*Surgery*
Medicine Cabinets	*The Lancet*
The Midwest	*American Demographics*
Mineral Oil	*New England Journal of Medicine*
Miniblinds	U.S. Consumer Product Safety Commission
Mobile Homes	University of Florida
Molasses	U.S. Food and Drug Administration
Mondays	American Association of Suicidology
Money	*Journal of the American Medical Association*; *Journal of Forensic Sciences*
Monster Truck Shows	United Press International
Morning Coffee	Duke University Medical Center
Mornings	*Stroke;* U.S. Centers for Disease Control and Prevention
Mouthwash	*Consumer Reports*; U.S. Consumer Product Safety Commission
Movie Previews	Washington University School of Medicine
Movie Theater Seats	*New England Journal of Medicine*
Mowing the Lawn	*American Journal of Cardiology*; Mayo Clinic
Mulch	*Journal of Occupational and Environmental Medicine*
Munchies	American Academy of Family Physicians
Museums	Johns Hopkins University
Mushrooms	U.S. Centers for Disease Control and Prevention
Mustaches	Mid-Atlantic Kaiser Permanente Medical Group
Nail Biting	*American Family Physician*
Nail Guns	*Journal of Trauma*
Napping	*Archives of Internal Medicine*
Narcissists	*Journal of Personality and Social Psychology*
Nevada	*Suicide and Life-Threatening Behavior*
New Clothes	*Environmental Science & Technology*
New Jersey	Automobile Association of America
New York City	University of California, San Diego; *Atlantic Monthly; Discover*

Nightclub Floors	*British Medical Journal*
Night Lights	*Nature*
Nightmares	*New Scientist*
Night Shifts	American Academy of Family Physicians; National Highway Traffic Safety Administration; National Center on Sleep Disorders Research
Nighttime	U.S. Bureau of Justice
North Carolina	U.S. Centers for Disease Control and Prevention; *American Demographics*
Nutmeg	Center for Addiction and Mental Health
Offices	Occupational Safety and Health Administration
Olive Oil	*Arteriosclerosis, Thrombosis and Vascular Biology*
Online Investing	ABC News
Opera	Royal Automobile Club
Parakeets	*Postgraduate Medicine*
Parsley	U.S. Centers for Disease Control and Prevention
Party Favors	U.S. Consumer Product Safety Commission
Party Lights	*British Medical Journal*
Paved Roads	*Internal Medical News*
Peppermints	Medical News Tribune Service
Percolated Coffee	Johns Hopkins Health Insider
Personal Computers	Cornell University; American Optometric Association
Personal Stereos	*The Lancet*
Photocopying	Columbia University
Picking Your Nose	Chicago Reader
Playgrounds	National Program for Playground Safety
Playing Rock and Roll	*USA Today*
Pogo Sticks	U.S. Consumer Product Safety Commission
Popcorn	*Journal of the American Medical Association*; Popcorn Institute
Popping Out of a Cake	*Daily Record*
Posturing	*Health*
Potato Guns	*Ophthalmology*
Powdered Latex Gloves	Public Citizen Health Research Group
Power Windows	*Auto and Road User Journal*
Prescriptions by Mail	Association of Pharmaceutical Scientists
Produce Sections	*New York Times*

Public Speaking	*Journal of Personality and Social Psychology*; East Tennessee State University
Pumping Iron	American Academy of Orthopaedic Surgeons
Pumpkin Carving	*New England Journal of Medicine*
Quitting Smoking	*Nature*
Racquet Sports	*Physician and Sportsmedicine*
Rain	*Men's Health*
Raw Milk	*American Journal of Public Health*
Recliner Chairs	U.S. Consumer Product Safety Commission
Red Food	University of Michigan Medical School
Red Kidney Beans	U.S. Food and Drug Administration
Refrigerator Magnets	U.S. Consumer Product Safety Commission
Religion	*Review of Religious Research*
Remote Controls	U.S. Consumer Product Safety Commission
Renting	*The Lancet*
Restaurant Meats	*ScienceDaily*
Retail Sales Jobs	U.S. Department of Labor
Riverside, California	Surface Transportation Policy Project
Rock Concerts	*Journal of the American Medical Association*
Roses	Johns Hopkins Health Information
Runways	Federal Aviation Administration
Salad Mixes	*Health*
Sandboxes	kidsource.com
Saturdays	*Accident Facts*, National Safety Council
Scary Movies	University of Michigan; University of Wisconsin
Seafood	U.S. Food and Drug Administration; U.S. Centers for Disease Control and Prevention
Shadowy Streets	University of California at San Diego
Shoes	American Orthopaedic Foot and Ankle Society; U.S. Consumer Product Safety Commission
Shopping Carts	U.S. Consumer Product Safety Commission
Shortness	Harvard Medical School; Brigham and Women's Hospital; *American Journal of Epidemiology*
Short Skirts	American Cancer Society
Singing in the Choir	*Audiology*
Sixteen-Year-Old Drivers	Insurance Institute for Highway Safety
Ski Wax	*Annals of Emergency Medicine*

Slam Dancing	*New England Journal of Medicine*
Slam Dunks	American Dental Association
Sleep	American Family Physician
Sleeping Bags	U.S. Consumer Product Safety Commission
Sleepless Nights	*American Journal of Hypertension*
Slow Cookers	U.S. Consumer Product Safety Commission
Small Heads	*Neurology*
Sneezes	*Health; Men's Health*
Snoring	University of California at Los Angeles School of Dentistry
Soap Operas	*British Medical Journal*
Socks	U.S. Consumer Product Safety Commission
Soundtracks	*Journal of General Psychology*
Sour Candies	*Self*
The South	U.S. Centers for Disease Control and Prevention; *Greensboro News & Record*
Soy	*Allergy*
Spain	*Eurosurveillance*
Sports Drinks	*British Journal of Sports Medicine*
Spring	American Association of Suicidology
Squirrels	*Atlantic Monthly*
Stemming Tears	Harvard Medical School
Stethoscopes	*Archives of Internal Medicine*; *The Lancet*
Stiff Palms	Yale University School of Medicine
Stiletto Heels	American Orthopaedic Foot and Ankle Society
Stone Floors	Reuters
Stools	U.S. Consumer Product Safety Commission
St. Patrick's Day	National Highway Traffic Safety Administration
Street Food	U.S. Food and Drug Administration
Stress Tests	Mayo Clinic
Strong Hands	*Arthritis and Rheumatism*
Stuffed Animals	*Discover*
Sugar Cane	*British Medical Journal*
Sugar-Free Gum	U.S. Food and Drug Administration
Summer	United Nations' Intergovernmental Panel on Climate Change
Sunglasses	*Health*
Sunlight	Johns Hopkins Wilmer Eye Institute
Sunscreen	*Journal of the National Cancer Institute*; American Academy of Dermatology

Topic	Sources
Sweethearts	Bureau of Justice
Swiss Cheese	U.S. Food and Drug Administration
Taj Mahal	Associated Press
Talcum Powder	American Health Foundation
Tallness	*Harvard Public Health Review*
Tanning Beds	Harvard School of Public Health; American Academy of Dermatology
Tap Water	*Epidemiology*; National Academy of Sciences; *International Journal of Environmental Analytical Chemistry*
Teahouses	U.S. Centers for Disease Control and Prevention
Telephones	U.S. Consumer Product Safety Commission
Telescopes	U.S. Consumer Product Safety Commission
Televangelism	Center for the Study of Religion/Spirituality
Television Sets	Radiological Society of North America
Thanksgiving	U.S. Food and Drug Administration; *U.S. News & World Report*
Therapy	National Institute for Occupational Safety and Health
Thin Thighs	Stanford University Medical School
Thunderstorms	*Journal of Epidemiology and Community Health*; National Oceanic and Atmospheric Administration
Tight Pants	American Academy of Dermatology
Toilets	U.S. Consumer Product Safety Commission
Tomato Sauce	U.S. Food and Drug Administration
Toothbrushes	University of Arizona
Toothpastes	*Nature*; U.S. Food and Drug Administration
Trampolines	*Pediatrics*; U.S. Consumer Product Safety Commission
Trying on Clothes	*New England Journal of Medicine*
Tug-of-War	United Press International
Tumbleweeds	Associated Press
Two-Lane Roads	Federal Highway Administration
Underpants Before Socks	Ohio Dermatological Association
Underwire Bras	*Washington Times*
Uneven Fingers	University of Liverpool; *New Scientist*
Urinals	International Paruresis Association
Vacuum Cleaners	U.S. Consumer Product Safety Commission; Environmental Protection Agency

Vegetarianism	*Physician and Sportsmedicine*
Vending Machines	*Journal of the American Medical Association*
Vigilance	*Health Psychology*
Visual Aids	*New England Journal of Medicine*
Volleyball	*Physician and Sportsmedicine*
Walking	*American Journal of Public Health*
Washing Dishes	U.S. Consumer Product Safety Commission
Watches	U.S. Consumer Product Safety Commission
Watching Television	*Archives of Pediatrics and Adolescent Medicine*
Water Balloons	American Academy of Ophthalmology
Water Beds	U.S. Consumer Product Safety Commission
Water Parks	U.S. Consumer Product Safety Commission; *Journal of Trauma*
Watering the Lawn	U.S. Consumer Product Safety Commission
Waynes	*New York Times*; Associated Press
Weak Hands	*Journal of the American Medical Association*
Wearing Clothes	U.S. Consumer Product Safety Commission
Weekends	Arizona State University
Well-Done Meat	National Cancer Institute
Wheelchairs	National Institutes of Health
White Coats	*American Journal of Hypertension*
Winter	U.S. Centers for Disease Control and Prevention; Johns Hopkins Health Insider
Women in Labor	*Family Practice News*
Woodstoves	*International Journal of Epidemiology*
Woodworking	U.S. Consumer Product Safety Commission
Yard Sales	U.S. Consumer Product Safety Commission
Yard Work	*The Lancet*; National Safety Council
Yoga	*DEA Health & Fitness Source*
Yo-Yos	*British Medical Journal*
Zippers	U.S. Consumer Product Safety Commission